I0591964

Group Therapy

by Ashburton Writers Group

ISBN 978-0-473-59147-2

Published by Stacey Broadbent, New Zealand, 2021
All Rights Reserved

Cover design Julie Sergeant
Edited by Stacey Broadbent

Group Therapy

by Ashburton Writers Group

President's Foreword

This collection of short stories and poems, is written by our members, often in response to 'writing prompts' given in our monthly meetings. We have included the winning entries to the Ashburton Writers Group, 2021 Paper Plus Short Story Competition.

The Ashburton Writers Group has been running for over twenty years, amongst our members we have amateurs, hobbyists, professional and published writers. If there is anything to be learnt from these types of groups, it's that 'you cannot judge a book by its cover'. Beneath the surface of sweet and normal people whom, by day may be parents, grandparents, neighbours, friends, employees and bosses, lies a profusion of ideas, beliefs, dreams, love, warmth, passion and darkness, that line in the sand that you do not cross. Each month we hear new stories and poems that are full of humour, evil, occasional profanity and sexual innuendo. It is a wondrous thing.

Julie Fechney
President, Ashburton Writers Group

Our aim is to contribute all profits to charitable causes, this year's recipients being Hospice Mid Canterbury.

Hospice Mid-Canterbury provides support for those with a life-limiting illness, their family and their caregivers. All services are free and are available throughout the Ashburton district between the Rakaia and Rangitata Rivers.

One of their many services is recording life stories, clients enjoy being able to take the time to recount their memories with one of the biographers, and many find it a very therapeutic process. The finished product becomes a treasured memento for the person's family. Hospice Mid Canterbury is a registered Charitable Trust and an Associate Member of Hospice New Zealand.

"Our goal is to help people make the most of their lives; to live every moment in whatever way is important to them."

Contents

Changing Focus

by Coby Snowden

About Coby

My background is accounting. I have worked at many interesting companies and non-profit organisations. I am currently the Treasurer of the National Rifle Association of NZ as well as Treasurer for various shooting-related and community organisations.

Long-range target rifle shooting is my passion. I got into it in my forties by accident (via a work team-building exercise). The sport has given me so much in terms of confidence, has taught me patience and has given me opportunities to travel the world. Most importantly, I met my husband through the sport.

I am constantly faced with the firearm safety debates and feel sad about how our sport is intertwined with criminal activity in the eyes of lawmakers.

That is what gave me the inspiration for the story 'Changing Focus'.

Changing Focus

Jackie squeezed the trigger and immediately turned towards Steve. She'd met him before. But where? She tried not to stare as she searched through her memory; his green polo shirt was emblazoned with his club logos. What was he wearing when she met him? A suit maybe?

"Bullseye." Steve gave her a thumbs up. "Might sign you up as a member."

Behind her, Ben laughed. "Wow, beginner's luck, eh?"

"Let's see if my second shot is lucky too," she said, while thinking 'Oh, where do I know him from, his voice is familiar too.'

"It's not luck. You sure you haven't touched a rifle before?"

"I've never shot before. I hate rifles; I would never have tried it if it wasn't for this team building. I was happy just watching, but my boss made me." She turned around and smiled at Ben. "Glad you did."

"Looks like you might even beat me," Ben chimed in, looking through a pair of binoculars.

She took aim, peering through the tiny peephole. "The target looks blurry now."

"Take your time, make sure you think of nothing but the target. Take your eyes off the target and look around for a bit."

Jackie's eyes drifted away. To her right, another coach was helping Dion. He seemed to be doing okay. Ahead she spotted some Pukeko birds, their distinctive red beaks pecking the ground.

"Don't the Pukekos get scared of the noise?"

"Nah," he replied, "they're used to it. At the Avon range there would be sheep wandering about."

Avon! Yes! She suddenly remembered him in a police uniform. Gee, that was over twenty years ago. "Did you by any chance happen to be a cop in Avon?" she asked tentatively, not really expecting him to remember her.

He scanned her face and raised his eyebrows. "Mmm, maybe, depends who's asking. I was, but that was a long time ago."

Yes, that was a long time ago. She shivered as she recalled coming home from the movies; she was only fifteen, so it probably wasn't very late, but it was in the middle of winter, pitch dark and freezing cold. Her house was surrounded by police. Steve had stopped her on the driveway.

"What is going on?" she screamed.

"Sorry, dear, but you can't go in."

"But this is my house. What's happening? Who's in there?"

"We don't know. I'll get someone to take you to number fifteen; your mum is there, and you'll be safe. Wait here".

"Why are the windows open?" she gasped "Oh my God, they're all broken." It looked like a bomb had exploded from the inside.

Just then, another officer ran from the driveway and shouted: "Get her out of here!"

At the same time, another officer yelled, "Do we need an ambulance?"

Steve turned around, and Jackie bolted. It had only taken seconds to get from the bottom of the driveway to the kitchen entrance. Her body tightened as she saw the scene again. He was sitting on a stool, an empty whiskey bottle by his feet. She shivered as she recalled the chilly draught whipping through the house, empty shells scattered around the floor, and, most terrifying by far, seeing the rifle; its barrel pointing straight up.

"Let's try another shot." Steve jolted her back to the present. "Try to relax that right shoulder."

As Jackie unclenched her fists, she brought the rifle to her shoulder and focused her mind on centering the target through the sight. She fired, and the target went down for marking.

"Told you, beginners luck. Phew, thought you were going to beat me for a sec!" Ben said as the target reappeared.

"That was okay," Steve said, "but you yanked the trigger. Remember you just want a gentle squeeze."

"Did I hit the target?"

"Oh yes." Another one of his wide beams and thumbs up. "Try again." Then a second later. "Hang on, the wind has picked up, just wait for the flags to drop back."

Jackie kept her finger resting on the trigger and remembered the way that man's finger was shaking as he held the trigger.

"Go away, leave me alone," he had slurred.

She took a step closer, reached out her hands. "Give me that rifle." But he didn't move. "Please!"

She had heard some commotion behind her, but she kept her eyes fixed on his trigger finger. When he groaned and let out a whiskey-reeking belch, she leaped forward and grabbed the barrel with both hands. He was a big man but was still seated on the stool. Jackie stood over him, keeping her eyes on his bloodshot eyes which were darting between her and the door. With both pairs of hands firmly around the warm barrel, she fought to keep her own panic hidden and managed a breezy, "Come on, don't be silly, let go."

But he kept his tight grip, yelling obscenities at the door. Jackie dared not look behind her. He was by now pulling the barrel towards him, and panic really set in when she noticed the end of the barrel was leaning against his throat. She pulled it with all the strength she could muster, using the legs of the stool for extra leverage. The rifle started to shift towards her, but suddenly he stood up, and as she stumbled backwards the rifle jerked and bounced back towards him, followed by an earsplitting bang. The bullet went through the kitchen ceiling. He froze as he met her eyes, and she swiftly wrenched the firearm from his hands. By then Steve was at her side and two other cops were dragging him away. "That was a brave but stupid thing to do young lady." He held out his arms for the rifle.

She threw it at him: "I never want to touch one of these bloody things again in my life."

But that was a long time ago.

"You're shooting very well, Jackie," said Steve, "how do you feel now? Still dislike rifles?"

"Well, it seems safe here, but plenty of criminals have them, they're awful weapons, victims have no chance. You must have seen some horrible sights as a cop."

"Oh yes, but I have also seen great community spirit and criminals turning their lives around. It wasn't all bad." He looked at her and winked. "I've also seen amazing bravery."

She took another shot, then studied the rifle she was holding. Wow, she was actually handling a lethal weapon, shooting real bullets.

"How do you know any of these shooters in your club aren't criminals?"

Steve laughed. "We do have some interesting characters." His voice became serious. "Every person here is passionate about our sport and wouldn't dream of harming anyone or risk confiscation of their firearms licences. Some of these guys–and ladies–represent New Zealand internationally. It's a great sport."

"I don't think my eyesight is good enough to take this up," said Jackie.

"You don't need perfect vision, it's more up here," Steve said, tapping his forehead. "As soon as you started shooting I could see you would be good. You had good focus and kept your cool with your boss right behind you. And I remember you keeping your cool when you were younger too, right?"

She did enjoy the thrill whenever Steve yelled out "bullseye." This rifle was used for sport, not danger. Maybe she finally found a sport she could be good at.

She fired her tenth shot and when the target reappeared asked, "What's my total score?"

While Steve scanned the scoresheet, she glanced at him and realised his life has changed too somewhat, from arresting bad guys using rifles as weapons to teaching firearm safety and target shooting. Teaching people from all walks of life, including victims of crime.

"42 out of a possible 50, that's really good for your first time." Steve beamed.

Ben wasn't smiling though. "Oh man, she beat me by five points," he groaned.

Jackie stood up, feeling ten foot tall, and this time gently handed Steve the rifle.

"Thank you so much for your help, Steve, how do I join the club?"

In this Neighbourhood

by Coby Snowden

From Coby

This poem came about from a prompt for one of the writers group meetings: "In the Neighbourhood".

I moved from Wellington to Ashburton in 2008, with absolutely no clue what life on a Mid Canterbury (or any!) farm would be like. I doubt many who work in CBD Wellington would appreciate the passion and indeed the struggles of farm life.

If, back then, someone told me I would be in amongst a rural community's worst nightmare, I would have laughed it off. I was a hot-shot finance manager at a large organisation, why would I give that up for life as a farmer's wife??

The answer, of course, is love.

In this Neighbourhood

In this neighbourhood folk are tired and worn down
It's been a month of heartbreak and hard slog
Mountains of sympathy from those living in town
For those unfortunate souls stuck in a muddy bog.

In this neighbourhood politicians showed sombre faces
Promises were given into reporters' steady lenses
While arable paddocks completely gone in some places
And farmers are still repairing or replacing fences.

Pup Chamberlain drives around with watchful ears
Carefully asking the expected: Are You Okay?
Rising suicide rates are among our biggest fears
What's the alternative, just pack up and walk away?

Kind strangers leave cooked meals by back doors
I hope they realise how that gesture means so much
Maybe the government will, next time it pours,
Offer more money for uninsured land and such.

In this neighbourhood things are already tough
And there's more laws prescribing farmers what to do
In this neighbourhood we scream Enough is Enough!
Policy makers in city offices just don't have a clue.

In this neighbourhood folk are tired, so tired
Of winter, rain, and unworkable stupid laws
Of hearing their career is the least admired
And battling constant environmental wars.

In this neighbourhood the ground hasn't yet dried
Some farmers struggle but make out they can cope
Will they once again be regarded with pride?
In this neighbourhood there is dwindling hope.

Unrequited Love

by Coby Snowden

Unrequited Love

Your demeanour says you truly are unaware
Just how much your existence means to me
I'm just a friend, a bloody good one to be fair
And have been for two decades, nearly three.
I loved you.

We've known each other since primary school
On my first day you grabbed my hand and heart
Showed me around, I thought you were so cool!
And over the next five years we were hardly apart.
I loved you.

College years were the best, just us and our mates
I passed exams, but you didn't do so well in class
When I wasn't helping you improve your grades
We'd go hiking, fishing or smoke some dodgy grass
I loved you.

While I studied law you went to an Aussie mine
Unbearable was the pain of being away from you
But then you totally broke me last Christmas time

When you returned home with a tan, and a wife too.
I hated you.

I'd never felt so gutted, my chances gone for real
So I got married too, trying to live a life of bliss
He's a good-hearted bloke, and we may seem ideal
But I dream of you, wanting your body, your kiss
I love you.

You keep coming over, I can see you're puzzled
My husband wonders why around you I'm cold
But I fight to keep my true feelings muzzled
It's a losing battle, I'd rather it was out, truth be told
I still love you.

How much longer do I wait? Do you feel the same?
Did you marry Anne to please your mum and dad?
I once heard them say your gayness was just a game
You'd "grow out of it" and forget about that Brad
But our love cannot die.

Christmas

by Coby Snowden

Christmas

I am dreaming of a relaxed Christmas
With my children behaving like angels
No guilty thoughts of diets or fitness
And no mention of anything contagious.

A huge hot meal in the middle of the day
Prepared it with much anxiety and fuss
It's just a friggin' roast, why go out of our way
Nigella's fancy gravy is not necessary for us.

I'm sooo looking forward to the day after
No more rushing around shops buying stuff
No more annoying music or the hoho laughter
From an overdressed fat man with white fluff.

And I can then take down the ridiculous tree
Vacuum the fake pine needles and fake snow
List the ugly unwanted presents on TradeMe
Then relax, sip leftover wine and wait for 2021 to show.

Corona

by Coby Snowden

Corona

Well, this year isn't turning out how it's meant to be
Did anyone forecast this, the whole world diseased?
We didn't panic about Wuhan, but Spain and Italy?
So we locked quickly, Air New Zealand not pleased.

Before lockdown, my calendar had lots of events planned
A musical, birthday parties, sporting trips away
But anything involving fun was well and truly banned
And in our boring, but safe, houses we had to stay.

Even very important people had to follow that rule
But the Minister of Health didn't like to be totally locked
He went for long bike rides far, and then, the fool
Was pretty mean to Ashley and now his career is totally focked.

The combined word for home and family became "bubble"
And, like a blister, popping it too soon was at your own peril

Going to the supermarket was just too much friggin trouble
With fellow shoppers in the loopaper aisle going feral.

So I resorted to opening cans well beyond best-by dates
From the bottom of the freezer chiselled plastic bags of meat
Tried recipe suggestions from Facebook mates
Using ingredients on hand, 'twas no mean feat.

Biscuit and cake-tins filled and emptied the same day
One day this mum went on a twenty-four-hour strike
Cries of "I'm hungry, and bored" I said "go away!"
"See what's left in the veggie garden, then get on yer bike".

Endless Stuff articles and of doom and gloom
The word of the year became "unprecedented"
Constant requests of get-togethers on Zoom
From Facebook friends I thought I had unfriended.

But I did learn a lot, had lots of time to read and think
Useful snippets of facts which can help us now, and later
Like, I used to think the dryer made my clothes shrink
But figured out it is probably, actually, the refrigerator
There are nineteen hundred and twenty steps, says my Fitbit

From our backdoor along the drive to the end of our
farm
Which included 12 minutes of walking through cowshit
But oh, quality me-time, kept me sane and calm

Relax and make the most of this time, they did say,
With your precious children at home pre-winter
Sorry, but I didn't cope too well with the endless
display
Of origami things made with paper from my work
printer

So, it was a great opportunity to do those tasks and jobs
We keep putting off till we have that elusive spare time
Sorting, filing, archiving, biffing junky bits and bobs
And six weeks should be long enough to rid my house
of grime

I could clean the greasy bit up above the rangehood
Tidy up the kitchen, sort out the Tupperware stack
Clean all the cupboards and pantry, yes, I could!
But, very soon, I got tired and the motivation never
came back

Then school term started, and I had to wear a teacher
hat
Expecting my girls to do their schoolwork without a
fuss

But everything was online this, online that, Kahoot, what's that?

Oh how I longed to once again see the driver of the school bus.

I had learnt their logins and passwords by week three

For their emails, online classrooms and numerous apps

Any money we had saved, like petrol or going out for tea

Went on extra data, and for the teacher a weekly bottle of schnapps.

But every day at 1, we tuned in to hear the of Director of Health

Give us good news, well, it was good compared to across the ditches

But Simon was too concerned about the reduction of wealth

His views pissed off lots of people, so it was Goodbye Mr. Bridges

Now, rather than counting cases of Covid 19

The news has switched to other numbers giving us a fright

We hear about the number of people escaping from quarantine

And how many National MPs have resigned tonight...

And now my life's back to normal, yes? Well, I guess

I can yet again buy a cappuccino at my favourite café

The girls back at school so the house is no longer a mess
And we can go out for tea any night (but not a buffet)

But...I kinda liked not having the early mornings rushed
And staying in bed till eight, eight thirty, even nine
I kinda miss not having to go out with my hair brushed
And as for coffee, instant Nescafe was just fine.

The virus has certainly changed our normal way of life
And to finish, I wish you all the best of luck
As for the missing tourists and National taking a dive
Frankly my dear, I don't give a damn

Unrequited Love

by Heather Sylvawood

About Heather

Heather Sylvawood's working life has revolved around writing and education, but only recently has she followed her earlier dreams of writing for pleasure.

She has self-published two novels, a collection of short stories and two books on her and her wife's experiences buying, renovating and selling real estate.

Her work is available on Amazon ebooks:

https://www.amazon.com/author/heathersylvawood

Unrequited Love

How we laughed at the beds,
Mismatched, uncomfortable and yet …
Dry, at least on that miserable West Coast day.
He laughed deeply at the joy of it
And I joined in the laughing
Though inside, I ached deeply.
It was on his bucket list, he'd told me.
Would I come? As a friend, you understand.
His voice laid the rules down clearly.
And fool that I was I said yes, eagerly.
I was to be the driver, he the passenger
Plumped into comfort with pillows.

We stopped frequently
To ease his pain, from limbs cramped
by the Asian space of the rental car.
Yet our conversation was buoyant.
He laughed at oddities on the trip:
Lambs on the wrong side of fences,
Trees bent to the prevailing wind.
Ordinary things that I didn't think extraordinary,

except when I saw them through his eyes.
I felt in myself hope rise bubbly, joyous;
Maybe now, he might come to see me differently.
His disease, he'd explained,
Had contorted his limbs without mercy;
Had robbed him of a future;
Friendship was all he had to give.
I wanted to shower him with words of hope,
To wrestle despair from his head;
To lie beside him and show him it wasn't so.

By the time we reached the township
The heavens had opened and driving was perilous.
"That's far enough," he said. "I've made the Coast,
Now let's find somewhere to stay."
Only three letters of the sign actually blinked.
He said: "It's a Mol, somewhere to go underground."
I laughed far more than the joke needed,
But I was tired, wanted to rest my eyes from the glare.
A well-padded woman, rose reluctant from her television,
Came shuffling, her eyes still riveted to the box.
Yes they had a unit, with cooker, fridge, and shower.
"It might fit a wheelchair," she told us, doubt clouding her voice.
But it was the beds that gave us the greatest delight:
One was hard and new and the other soft and sinking.
He said: "I'll take the soft one to cushion my limbs."

Then he warned: "You'll have to lift me out come morning."

"A small price to pay," I said, though I didn't say what for.

Both weary, we prepared for bed, lifted cups of cocoa to the bucket list day ahead, and climbed under the covers.

"Good night," I called, but he was already snoring

It was the stillness that woke me early.
Quiet, oh so quiet.
I stopped breathing and listened but
I could not still the rushing of my heart.

The men from the ambulance lifted him gently
from the deep indentation in the mattress.
Transferred him to the flashing vehicle and
stole him away. In the silent motel room all
I wanted was to crawl into the shape of him
For one first cuddle; for one last one.
It was that impression of him that spilled my tears –
The loss of him etched in the mattress.
Love.
Gone.
Left unrequited.

The Other Side of Christmas

by Heather Sylvawood

The Other Side of Christmas

Their father said he couldn't come,
His car was in the garage.
"You know, I would've if I could've," he said
Then added: "You know that, don't you, Katy-girl?"
He used his pet name for me, like
Hoping that I'd cave in,
As I so often had.

I let the silence fall between us,
As I so often did, and thought:
"One less face at the table,
One less set of gifts for the kids."
Though the cynical part of me said:
"Saves him spending on them."
"So I'd better go," he tried again.
"I'll see ya'll when I'm next in town.
"Tell them Dad loves and misses them."
"K," was all I said.
I didn't feel like fleshing out the lie.

He would not come. He was not there.

I told the kids on Christmas Eve.
They flinched then held it in.
"Oh well," Melody said, though Susy cried.
Nick grunted and went back to his console.
When my parents heard, they said:
"Well, we'll come over—make up the numbers."
And for the first time they came for Christmas:
Mum, bearing carefully knitted hot water bottle covers;
Dad, handing out last-minute purchases of sweets.

In the evening on Christmas Day
I made them bedtime Milo,
With marshmallows floating on the top.
As usual, Susy spilled hers on the carpet
And Melody scolded, as she often did.
Nick just sat and flicked his thumbs on console keys.
And even though it was too warm outside
I filled their new hotties, warm with love.
"Go off to sleep, my little peeps," I said
"Tomorrow is another day,
On the other side of Christmas."

The Silence of Christmas

by Heather Sylvawood

The Silence of Christmas

Our teacher, she said, "write a poem,
A poem about Christmas."
Later she toured the class
To see what we had written.

"Why haven't you written anything, Nathan?" she
asked.
So I told her blunt: "I hate Christmas."
She drew back, all shocked, like no one
Could ever not like Christmas.
Her words move her body into brittle
Like my Dad's, after a beer or two.
Though she didn't raise her fists,
She just said, in careful beats:
"Why don't you like Christmas?"

I felt my eyes sting with tears,
Gulped air into my lungs,
Choked on the pain in my throat.
I could not find the words to say:

Christmas makes my mum cry.
My Dad's anger rises as the beer bites.
My sister and big brother slam out the door
Trapping a shadow of rage in the room.
Blinking, blinking the plastic lights shine
On torn scraps of wrapping paper from
Disappointing promises.
And, if I'm not quick enough,
I'll feel his fists rake my face.
"What's the matter with you, fuck-wit?"

So I retreat into silence.

2021 Paper Plus Short Story Competition Winners

11 years and Under

My Dream Come True

by Sylvie France

My Dream Come True

The sun rays shone through my dull curtains as my eyes adjusted to the daylight. Pulling my robe on, I scuffed my feet into my slippers. I pulled the curtains to the side as I emerged onto the rickety balcony of the old farmhouse.

It had been a year since my dad had passed and Mum and I had moved to the country, but it still felt like we moved in yesterday.

In the distance I could see a dust cloud approaching. "Cuz!" Millie yelled, her long hair blowing in the wind, as she skidded to a stop on her four-wheeler. "Pull some joddies and a tee on," she yelled, "the dairy cows and horses aren't going to feed themselves."

It was a month until the Grand Prix show jumping competition and tension was growing. Millie was riding two of the best stable horses; Ray of Sunshine and Circo. It was my dream to ride in a Grand Prix show jumping competition, but the head of the stables, Mike, said I had to prove myself first.

Setting myself to work, I fed all the horses, pausing to spend some time with Circo. Circo's velvet muzzle nuzzled my cheek as she ate the sugar cubes from my damp fingers.

The next few weeks flew by in preparation for the Grand Prix show jumping champs. Each day I rode all the trekking, dressage and games horses. I was distraught when Mike told me that Millie would be riding Circo in the lead up to the jumping season.

My alarm rang well before daylight. Once we got to the showgrounds I set to work, polishing the horses to perfection.

"Now in the ring can we have Millie Jones, riding Ray of Sunshine!" the loud speaker boomed. Millie cantered into the ring, approaching the first jump with aggression. They flew over. The next few jumps went in a blur, but as they approached the last jump, Ray of Sunshine shied. Millie went flying, hitting the jump with speed! Millie screamed as she clutched her leg…

Mike turned to me. "August, get Circo and warm him up. You will be riding him." As I warmed her up, I focused fully on Circo changing paces, jumping each warm-up jump. We were the last ones to go. I leaned down and whispered in Circo's ear, "This is our chance to shine."

There's Only One Mission

by Jack Gorrie

There's Only One Mission

2035, seven years after the last signal from the Europa Clipper mission, NASA's Ariel Clipper is about to insert into orbit around Uranus.

This all started as a routine, planetary orbital surveying mission. The launch was perfect. The gravity assist flyby of Mars was perfect. That all changed after the Jupiter system flyby. NASA had planned for the retired Europa Clipper spacecraft to upload telemetry from the onboard CPU. The two machines were supposed to "shake hands." But something was buried in that message. It had placed Ariel Clipper and i's artificial intelligent system into critical safe mode. Something in the download; Europa had taken over Ariel's artificial intelligence. NASA had lost control.

For six years ... silence.

NASA could only hope that the Clipper would follow its pre-programmed flight path. Weeks and months had passed. Everyone back on Earth was expecting some sort of signal from Uranus. Some sign that the mission was still alive. The main power booster seemed to have frozen; all hope was lost... When suddenly, a green light appeared on one of the computers at the NASA HQ directing them to turn on their big screen. Ariel Clipper bursts out of its self-imposed coma, two hours and 45 minutes after NASA received a signal. The message was totally unexpected.

It was an image file.

Line by line, canyons, and ridges, fault scraps, and craters all appeared on the main screen at NASA's communication headquarters.

It was a selfie! Better yet, it was a "double selfie".

Everyone cheered with laughter as they saw the main body of the clipper spacecraft, with the tiny moon Ariel in the background. For some reason this plucky little spacecraft had disobeyed its original program and locked itself in on the little moon Ariel, a small dust ball in space. No pictures of Oberon. No pictures of Titania.

Then, slowly scrawling across the screen appeared a simple line.

"Europa told me, it's lonely out here. So I decided to go find my friend... Ariel."

Murder Mystery

by Audric Chai

Murder Mystery

Cody Brown raced down a narrow alleyway dodging loose crates and boxes like a parkour ninja. Following close behind were his best friends Cooper and Carter Beckett. 'Troublemakers' is how their parents would describe them. The team had plans to visit an abandoned fossil digging site hoping to click some pictures for a school project.

"So much for amazing fossils, Cody," said Cooper. "There isn't a single bone in sight!"

"Patience, Coop, patience," Cody breathed.

"Patience? We've been waiting for an hour. How much longer do you want?" exclaimed Carter. Then there came a loud noise like gears shifting places.

"What was that?" Cody whispered when the sound stopped abruptly. Carter just shrugged his shoulders.

Suddenly, the ground dropped beneath them into a deep pit, and Cody felt all the breath knocked out of his lungs and the grit grinding in his teeth. Then every sound in the digging site came to a halt. Cody told himself to calm down and that everything was going to be okay, so he was nearly starting to feel normal until he looked below him. The revolting, nauseating sight below him made his heart stutter to a stop like a train coming to the end of its track. What he saw underneath him was a deceased body, covered in flies and rotting flesh.

"Um, it's alright guys, just… just stay calm," Cooper stuttered, but Cody didn't feel anything near calm, and he didn't think anyone else felt it either.

After ten minutes or so, they managed to painstakingly dig their way out of the pit and when they looked back down at the bottomless pit and the body, they then knew that something more would have to happen. "I don't think it can get any closer than that!" said Cooper.

"C'mon! You just—" Cody didn't have time to finish his sentence before a person started yelling at them. "—jinxed it…" Cody finished, staring in shock at the figure holding a knife behind them. Cody heard voices yelling his name as he jerked his head up from his pillow to be greeted by his mum screaming loudly in his ear to wake up and get out of bed.

When Cody's mum calmed down, she asked him, "Why don't you go to the digging site with your friends for the school project?"

Cody took a deep breath and shouted in disbelief, "Not again!"

Corona

by Stacey Broadbent

About Stacey

Stacey resides in Ashburton, New Zealand with her husband and three children. She is a qualified proof-reader, author, wife, mother, and self-proclaimed culinary goddess. When she's not busy writing or editing books, she enjoys reading and procrastinating on TikTok.

She absolutely loves hearing from readers, so please feel free to reach out via email, Instagram, or join her reader group, Broadbent's Bookish Babes. You can also sign up to her newsletter for up-to-date info on releases.

www.staceybroadbent.weebly.com
Stacey Broadbent
Author

www.facebook.com/StaceyBroadbentAuthor
www.amazon.com/staceybroadbent

Corona

"Please tell me you haven't been sitting there all morning." Alfie sighs as he sits across from his wife. A slight twitch to her lips is the only sign she's heard him, but she doesn't move from her spot. Her forgotten coffee sits on its coaster where he placed it two hours earlier. "Have you at least eaten, love?"

She snorts, turning two beady eyes towards him. "Who can eat at a time like this?" She turns back to the window, her nose mere centimetres from the glass.

Alfie clears his throat, shuffling his seat closer and sliding a hand across the table. "I know this whole lockdown thing is a little scary, but we don't have to stay indoors. How about we go outside? Have a little walk around the streets? I hear people are putting bears up in the neighbourhood for the kids to find. Why don't we see if we can spot them?" His fingers brush against her elbow, and she glares at him.

"Go out there? With all of them?" she demands. "You're out of your mind, Alfie. You haven't seen what they've been doing out there. It's madness!" She tugs at the binoculars hanging around her neck. "This coronawhatsit is doing things to their minds." She taps her forehead. "Making them crazy."

"I don't think it works that way, love. People are just doing what they can to keep the boredom at bay."

Agnes tuts, pulling the binoculars from her neck and handing them to Alfie. "Just you look." She points out the window. "Across there. That woman has been out in her front yard in at least ten different outfits since this morning. Ten, Alfie! She's been jumping in and out of bushes, rolling around on the ground, talking to herself." She shakes her head. "Poor thing is falling apart."

"I don't know," Alfie says as he holds the binoculars to his eyes. "She doesn't look crazy to me. Maybe she's making one of those tic-tac things the news was talking about the other night. Some new video thing the young ones are doing."

"Don't be so silly, Alfie. She's lost the plot. She has the corona."

"Well, look over there." He points to a couple in matching tracksuits, walking briskly down the street. "They look perfectly normal to me, and they're outside in the fresh air. Look, they even waved at her." He turns to his wife with a smile. "It can't be that bad out there."

She huffs and rolls her eyes. "They've been past three times already today. They don't stop, Alfie. They just keep walking around and around. I'm telling you. The people in this neighbourhood are going downhill fast. I'm not going out there and letting it get me too."

She folds her arms across her chest, shaking her head. "No, thank you."

"It can't get you unless you're in contact with someone who's sick though, Agnes."

"That's what they want you to think! I've been listening though. It's those microwaves or some such. We're all just breathing it in, and then it takes over your brain." She waves her hand towards the window. A man clad in Lycra bends and stretches. "See? It's just not natural, Alfie. Who in their right mind would do that?"

"I think they're just trying to get fit, love."

"Hogswash. No one exercises of their own free will. I'm telling you, Alfie, it's not normal." She takes up the binoculars and turns back to the window. "That's why we have to stay vigilant and keep watch. That corona won't get past me. You can bet on it."

Christmas Fun

by Stacey Broadbent

Christmas Fun

'Twas the week before Christmas, and all through the house,
Wallets once bulging were now flattened down.

A second mortgage taken, and a loan for your soul,
Just so you can buy that Swarovski bowl.

It takes pride of place on your table so fancy,
All to outdo your nemesis, Nancy.

There's glitter and tinsel and baubles galore,
And even a wreath adorning your door.

But Nancy has reindeer, a sleigh and some canes.
Her house is lit up like a runway for planes.

So back to the store you trudge, all a wary,
To find one more thing; perhaps a gold fairy.

You make your way home with your arms overflowing,
To one up your neighbour by making it snowy.

You aim the machine at your lawn all aglow,
And slowly start spreading a layer of snow.

But the trigger gets stuck and the sprayer won't stop,
And snow fires out at 100 knots.

It covers the windows, the gardens and deck.
And still it keeps going till you cry, "Bloomin' heck!"

And Nancy comes running to see what's the matter.
To see why you're making a terrible clatter.

She grabs for the gun, and you wrestle together,
To wrangle the weapon that's causing this weather.

It comes to a stop with a godawful splutter,
But not before filling all of the gutters.

You turn to Nancy with eyes open wide,
As you notice the chaos has spread to her side.

You've gone overboard, you had such a nerve,
So you brace for the scolding you rightly deserve.

But Nancy just smiles and her shoulders she shrugs,
And then she starts laughing and gives you a hug!

"Merry Christmas," she says as she waves her goodbye,

Heading back to her home with a glint in her eye.

And you watch with confusion, a frown on your face.
Could it be that this whole thing was never a race?

There was no competition, no fight with dear Nancy.
She really just wanted her house to look fancy.

It was all in your head, a game for the season,
Made into a fight, with no rhyme and no reason.

Who Am I?

by Stacey Broadbent

Who Am I?

Folding my gangly legs beneath me, I watched as Mum and Dad paced back and forth. It was never a good sign when they said they wanted to "have a talk". That was code for "you're in trouble". It didn't matter that the other kids teased me about being different all the time, I was meant to take the high road and not lash out. But sometimes it was too hard.

"Look, son, your mother and I feel it's time we told you the truth," Dad began, and my heart began to pound. I had no idea where this was going, and something told me I didn't want to know either. "There's no easy way to tell you this, but…" He looked to Mum who nodded, turning her glassy eyes away.

She couldn't even bare to look at me. I'd really done it this time. It was obvious what was going on. They'd finally had enough and wanted me to fly the coop, go out on my own…

"We've done the best we can for you, son, but we don't know how to take care of you anymore. You need to be with your own kind."

My head swam and my heart plummeted to my stomach. My own kind? What did that mean?

Dad glanced at Mum again, then back to me. "You must've noticed you're not like the rest of us." He nodded at my long neck and legs: the very things he knew I was sensitive about. The others taunted me daily, calling me stretch and rubber neck. I hated that I was different to the rest of them, but I couldn't change who I was.

I hunched up, tucking my neck into the folds to make me seem smaller. "I'm just big boned is all, right, Mum?" I turned to the one parent I knew would make me feel better.

"Honey," she started in her soft voice, fresh tears in her eyes. "It's not that. You're... you're..." Her voice broke and she turned away again.

"The truth is, son, we, ah, we don't really know who your real parents are."

"What?" I almost laughed. "What do you mean? You're my real parents."

"No, son, we're not."

"No, that's not true. Mum?" I pleaded. "Tell me that's not true."

"I'm sorry, honey, I can't." She waddled over to me, nestling her head against my neck. "We raised you, yes, and you are our son in our eyes, but we don't know who you came from."

"But... how?"

"Well, your father and I had been trying to have a baby for a very long time when we saw a fox run off with a nest one day, and an egg rolled out onto the path behind it, so we scooped it up and kept it safe and warm while we searched for the parents. But no one returned."

"So, I was the egg?"

"I'm afraid so."

"So, I'm not a duck like you?"

"No, son, you're a swan."

Mistake

by Stacey Broadbent

Mistake

I stare at the disarray surrounding me. "Oh no. I think I've made a terrible mistake."

I blame BookTok of course. Before I discovered a world of others as obsessed with books as I am, I had been blissfully unaware of the beautiful home libraries and shelf designs people had. But now, it's all I see, and it gave me the hairbrained idea to drag every book I own out into my little office to create my own little oasis of solitude.

Of course, I never realised just how many books I had until they were stacked in piles around me, awaiting their new home.

Now, with literally hundreds of books stacked on my desk, chair, and all over the floor, it's hard to know where to begin. I can barely move without knocking a pile over and starting an unfortunate domino effect.

The task suddenly seems monumental, but I'm past the point of no return. I must make it through to the other side or I'll be wading in books for the rest of my life.

But where do I begin? There is no beginning to this pile of madness. No end in sight either. Only an endless supply of books with myriad ways to display them.

Do I go by author? By series? Read and not read? Or how about book size? Genre? Or maybe that rainbow cover effect? Favourite books together? Signed books? Separate by country? The choices are endless!

"Oh god, what have I done?" I drop my head into my hands in despair. Then an idea hits me. It makes perfect sense. What's a new library space without new shelves? A trip to the store is in order for some much-needed retail therapy.

So, I grab my shoes and my purse, and I rush out the door to scour the stores for the perfect shelf to ease my suffering.

An hour later, I burst through the door with a grin on my face.

"Find what you needed?" Hubby asks.

And with a glint in my eye, I nod, presenting my new purchase.

Hubby raises an eyebrow but doesn't say a word as I cradle four new books against my chest. "They were buy one, get one half off. I couldn't' just leave them there."

"And the library?" he asks.

I wave a dismissive hand through the air. "I'll do it tomorrow."

Handle with Care

by Julie Sergeant

About Julie

I have enjoyed a variety of roles in different industries in the UK: Film and TV, Advertising and Design, the Motor Industry, Service and Hospitality. Four years as an airline flight attendant, enabled me to indulge my love of travel, although there are still a few places to tick off my bucket list.

After eighteen years in New Zealand as a freelance writer and editor of a local newspaper, I am now a quiet living, middle-aged, mother of two, who writes for pure pleasure.

I enjoy the magic of words; when spun together with the swish of an inked wand, they can entertain, captivate, amuse and scare the pants off people.

Handle with Care

Handle with Care is the label on the large brown box I fall over as I struggle through my front door. I couldn't see it through the bags of groceries I am juggling and just lugged up three flights of stairs to my apartment.

"Aaagh… What the??? …" My screams must have been heard; there is thundering up the stairs as Larry arrives wielding a baseball bat. James from across the street isn't far behind, and Jessie glides up from the ground floor, as only Jessie can, carrying her ever-present glass of red.

James, gorgeous front man of well-loved rock band Storm, smiles and holds his hand out to help me up. As I touch him for the first time, a glorious shiver runs up my spine. Stunned at this reaction, I can't seem to move and just stand there watching him picking up my groceries, which have scattered across the highly polished wooden floors. I notice his strong arms as he reaches under the sofa to retrieve the mayonnaise; imagining what they would feel like wrapped around me, I….

"Are you okay, Diana?" interrupts Larry as he nervously, and a little too enthusiastically, looks around my apartment for someone to bash.

Pulled out of my reverie, I feel the blush rise up through my neck and, a little annoyed, I respond sharply, "Yeah, I'm okay, Larry. I fell over that stupid box! Do you know how it got in here?"

If anyone would know, Larry would. He's a playwright, a confirmed bachelor and silver fox, spending most of his days in his apartment writing, and most nights out on the town, seducing women with his wit, celebrity stories and irresistible charm.

His inability to shed any light on the arrival of this box in my hallway, I turn to James and Jessie; their synchronised shaking of heads says no.

By now, like within a minute, half the residents of Pomander have arrived. Not much goes unnoticed on 'The Walk', something I both love and loath about our little village. The English Tudor inspired street, spanning one block of the Upper West Side of New York, is a hidden treasure, locked behind large iron gates. Pomander Walk has withstood the test of time and greedy developers, since 1922, it's residents past and present, going passionately into battle every time its existence comes under threat of destruction and replacement by a repugnant skyscraper.

Right now though, I'm becoming claustrophobic in my small apartment, as more neighbours arrive, drawn by the unfolding drama;

greeting each other warmly, they discuss their concern about the box's unnoticed delivery and arrival inside my apartment.

"Okay people!" I yell over the cacophony. "Thank you all for your concern, I'm fine, you can return home now."

The sudden silence is deafening, as everyone turns towards me. Jessie, quite drunk as she has been topping up her glass with an open bottle she found sitting on my benchtop, slurs what everyone is thinking...

"Aren't you going to open it? I want to know what's inside."

Ugghhh! Now I have to open it or they will pester me for days. It seems all concern about how the box got inside my apartment has been pushed aside by curiosity.

"Okay! Okay!" My hands up defensively as I squeeze through the throng. I take out the delivery note from its little plastic wallet on top, and sigh. "Oh, for heaven's sake, it's not even for me!"

"Jessie?!" I ask with as much patience as I can muster.

"Ooooh, is it for me?" she asks, no longer 'gliding', as she teeters towards me and the box. "Heaven's, I must have given the wrong apartment number, silly me! Hic!"

With a chorus of "open it, Jessie!" and delighted that she is the centre of attention, the infamous

Broadway actress makes the most of it, opening the box with as much drama as is humanly possible.

Everyone stops breathing in anticipation as they look into the box...

Larry looks at me, shaking his head. "It's wine. It's wine, isn't it?"

I look over Jessie's shoulder, and sure enough, nestled amongst the shredded paper are three tiny wooden crates, emblazoned with 'Fragile' and a wine glass icon.

Jessie is ecstatic, as she lifts the first little crate out and says, "Not just any wine, Larry, limited editions. This Grand Hermitage is one of only twenty bottles in existence, and the other two are equally as rare."

Amongst the chorus of 'oohs' and 'aaahs' around us, my annoyance gets the better of me, and I bite out rather sarcastically, "They won't be in existence long if you drink them, Jessie."

"Lord, no!! As much as I love a good wine, Diane, these are an investment. They are not for drinking."

A snort escapes from my face. "Next time you 'invest' in something so expensive, best you get it sent to the right address then!"

The show now over, everyone files out of my apartment. Larry helps Jessie up and says, "I'll take these down to your apartment for you, Jessie. Don't want your investments decorating the stairs."

Jessie, helping herself to another glass of my red, beams her red-carpet smile at him and says, "Thank you, Larry, you are such a darling."

Then she turns to me and grimaces. "May I recommend Gotham Wines for your future purchases? This is a little too 'grocery store' for my taste."

My chin hits the floor. 'Cheeky bitch!' I think, and I hear Larry laughing as he disappears down the stairs.

A Royal Pickle

by Julie Sergeant

A Royal Pickle

Oh no! What's happening? My loyal little car is making an awful chugging noise and slowing down; it really doesn't sound healthy.

"Keep going, pleeease keep going." I urge as I look through the windscreen at the white out ahead. But no, she slows painfully and then stops, and no amount of cajoling, threats or encouragement can get her started again.

I run my hands lovingly around the steering wheel. "My poor, old girl, you've seen me through thick and thin these last four years, but even you can't compete with this wild New Zealand weather."

I check my phone – no service. I'm in a right pickle now, stuck in the middle of nowhere, in a snowstorm, with no heat, no food and no way to call for help.

I have a decision to make. Get out and attempt to walk the six kilometres back to the village, possibly freezing to death. Or stay in the car, contemplate death by snowplough, and, of course, I could freeze to death. Great!

I look around for any signs of life; another vehicle, a light, a house, a barn. The falling snow making it impossible; I can hardly see the pine trees lining the far side of the road.

Okay, decision made... I put on every piece of clothing I have in the car, grab my torch from the glove box and, feeling somewhat like the Michelin Man, climb out into the cold. Sinking down into the fluffy, white snow, I am relieved it isn't yet deep enough to reach the top of my leather boots.

I turn and walk back in the direction of Becky's warm, cosy house; my old friend and new mum, unaware of my predicament in this unexpected storm. I come to a crossroads and look about, but there are no lights in either direction, no buildings that I can see, so I carry on. I look at my phone, hopeful; still no signal. "Bloody wopwops. Who in their right mind wants to live out here anyway!" My voice breaks the complete silence all around me, making me jump and then laugh at myself. It is getting harder to walk as the snow deepens and my boots and thermal socks become heavy with moisture. I am beginning to wish I had stayed in the car.

It is now fully dark, my torch barely lighting a few metres ahead, and it's eerily quiet. I realise that even if there is a house nearby, unless they have their outside lights on, I may miss it. I can't feel my legs, yet I know I am still moving at a crawl now as the cold is pushing its way through my layers of clothes like an unstoppable glacier. Time and space seem to stop around me. I could have been walking for a few minutes, it could have been hours. I feel my senses shutting down.

I have no idea how far I have walked as I approach the next crossroads and, despite having driven this road a hundred times, my surroundings feel totally unfamiliar, wrapped in its new cloak of white. I am very tired and starting to shiver; the urge to just lie down and have a nana nap is getting stronger. I know I mustn't; that will be the end of me. "Keep going. I'll just walk a few more metres, just a few more, and then I'll rest." My voice and the crunch of my boots the only sound in the night.

A faint buzzing starts in my head, it's annoying me. The noise then becomes a deep rumble, loud enough to penetrate my trance like state. Suddenly, I recognise the sound as a large diesel engine and look up just in time to see an enormous tractor turning away from me. My torch! My fingers are too frozen to use the on/off switch, so I can only wave the feeble light.

"Help! Help!" I yell as I frantically move my torch up and down and side to side, hoping the driver will notice me. I try to run, but my legs won't work.

The tractor doesn't stop, and as it pulls away, I realise that may have been my only hope of rescue. "That's it, I'm a gonner. I'll be a popsicle for a couple of days and thaw out with the snow before anyone finds me. Where's the knight on his trusty steed when you need him? I'm a damsel in distress after all."

I give up, sit down on the snow, chuckling to myself at the vision of a horse and knight in this weather, then I recall a phrase from Star Trek; 'resistance is futile'. Well that just about sums it up. I reflect on my short life and wonder who'll turn up to my funeral. My parents will be devastated of course, poor Mum and Dad. Will my tough guy of a brother, Josh, be able to hold it together for them or lose it? Becky will be there for them anyway; she is the most capable woman I know.

Damn, that buzzing again... I wonder if my high school friends will turn up; I haven't seen some of them for four years, and then there're the guys from work....

I can no longer keep my eyes open and feel myself drifting off.

I hear a gruff voice. I force my eyes open, and there it is; the enormous tractor, the door opened slightly and a voice shouting at me… "What the bloody hell do you think you are doing out here? I caught your torch light out of the corner of my eye. You're bloody lucky, stupid woman, being out in this weather!!"

How rude, I think to myself, but I am overwhelmed with relief so say nothing. He jumps down and stands over me, hands on his hips.

"I'm waiting for my knight in shining armour, but you'll do," I say with more gusto than I feel.

"Better get in then, my lady," he says, a little contrite perhaps. I try to get up, but I can't seem to coordinate my brain and my body. I hear an exasperated sigh and then I am lifted into the cab.

"Got no Darjeeling, I'm afraid, only coffee, if it'll please you?" he says as he gets in the driver's side.

It's pitch black, and I hardly recognise the face reflected back to me in the windscreen. What I see is not attractive; a pale face blotched with red raw patches, and although I can't feel it, I am smiling.

A rough hand passes me a steaming mug of coffee, the blast of air from the tractor's heater defrosts me just enough to hold it, and I drink the hot liquid gratefully, feeling its warmth spread through my body.

I turn and look to my saviour to say thank you and find a pair of concerned but amused, twinkly green eyes looking at me from a ruggedly handsome face.

"My car broke down. I wouldn't normally be out for a stroll in this weather. Thank goodness you found me, I was just about done in."

"At your service, Ma'am," he says doffing his imaginary cap. "My farm is the closest property. We need to get you dried out and warmed up before hypothermia sets in."

As he turns the wheel and we lurch forward, he glances sideways at me and, with a cheeky grin, says, "It's no palace, but it's all mine."

Aaaahhhh, I sigh gratefully, relaxing into the seat, "My Hero…"

Caroline's Journal

by Julie Sergeant

Caroline's Journal

February 1st

I felt really down today. It was hard to get through 'Children's Hour' at the library. Seeing all those gorgeous, wee preschoolers, their faces so animated, listening intently to Clare as she read to them.

I couldn't concentrate. Jackie Collins ended up shelved with the J's not C's, and I managed to print 40 copies of the wrong side of a customer's poster.

The last round of IVF is looking doubtful. Greg and I have been waiting patiently for a baby, and the last three years with Doctor Frampton has brought us no success. There doesn't seem to be any reason for our struggles, which makes it all the more frustrating.

Greg is putting on a brave face and trying to keep my spirits up, but I know he wants to chuck in the towel and try adoption. He is the last of his line, you see, the only Norfolk born Smythe left, and he desperately wants to see his name and business continue into the future.

Greg is a roofer by trade, not slate, tile or steel but thatched roofs, and his expertise is in very short supply. He travels the country creating and repairing thatched roofs for cottages and barns. He's well known to the Historical Society and those 'Keep Britain Quaint' nutters.

Anyway, better get dinner on the table. Greg's been to Kibworth Harcourt near Leicester today and the old fella that owns the place is one of the 'nutters' so Greg usually has a headache by the time he gets home. I've made his favourite; beef stew and dumplings.

February 12th

Been to see Doc Frampton today and he's confirmed the bad news; no babies. I watched Greg's face and I could see he was gutted but trying so hard to hide it. I'm not sure I could go through another round of injections, rising hopes and then disappointment. God only knows how Greg feels. I am going to bite the bullet and put a stop to it all now. We are still young enough to adopt a baby, more than one if we wanted. I am going to tell Greg when he gets home from Chedgrave. The old girls over there treat him really well, never short of a cuppa and piece of cake.

March 1st

Really excited as we are off to the Lake District, staying at our favourite place in the Hamlet of Troutbeck. Greg and I love the open spaces and gorgeous rolling, green hills; we go for long walks, play golf, do a bit of fishing, and last year we even had a go at waterskiing on Lake Ullswater. I managed to stand up twice. I was so proud. Greg took to it really quickly and had a wonderful time. I'm so happy to be spending four stress free days and nights in that magical place.

March 5th

Brilliant, it has been absolutely brilliant. Greg and I had a lovely time; the sun shone constantly, except at night of course, LOL. Oh, what is the matter with me? I am so all over the place. I obviously needed the break. I feel alive and full of energy.

Must have been all that hiking we did around Troutbeck, and we even managed to climb up to Sharp Edge on Blencathra. The view from up there was amazing. There were so many rabbits and hares bounding around, far more than usual. Greg kept shouting 'rabbit stew' and 'Mixamatosis'. I laugh but am normally a little embarrassed by his funny outbursts; an introvert, I don't usually do well in public. We sat and watched the rabbits whilst we had a cup of tea from the flask. Talk about 'Mad as a March Hare', they were dashing all over the place and jumping straight up into the air. Although I had read about 'boxing hares', I was totally unprepared for the spectacle. It wasn't very romantic, I can tell you, but then I am not a Jill hare; one look from one of those Jacks and I would have yielded without a fight.

They were all too busy to notice us, let alone fear us, and one gorgeous female came up and tried to nibble some of my sandwich. She had huge brown eyes full of compassion, and as I looked into them, breaking some bread for her, she touched my outstretched hand with her nose. I felt a warmth flood through my body, and then she hopped off. It was a strange and beautiful moment.

On the way back to the Inn, we went to the local shop for a silver spoon to add to my mum's collection. Greg picked up his usual golf and fishing magazines and paid for them before I made up my mind which spoon to get Mum. I ended up choosing the Mrs. Tiggy-Winkle teaspoon from the Beatrix Potter collection, I knew she didn't have that one. I got a present myself that day. Greg had found this beautiful silver necklace and thought it would remind us of our perfect day. He gave it to me later over dinner, and I haven't taken it off since.

March 29th

I went to see Doctor Frampton today. I have been feeling a little odd lately and just wanted to check I wasn't suffering any withdrawal side effects from the IVF treatment. He took a sample of blood and said he'd call in a couple of days, could just be my hormones settling or a lack of iron or something. Greg is home in about an hour. He has had a long trip today, down to

North Devon. Roast beef and Yorkshire pud should cheer him up.

March 30th

I am in shock, utter shock! I thought Greg was behaving a little odd tonight, suggesting we go to the local pub for a meal. He had some rare time at home today, no thatching needed until Monday. He was very romantic and constantly smiling. I went to order a red wine, almost salivating at the thought of that first sip. It's been so long going without; one of the sacrifices of IVF.

"No," he said with a wink to the barman, "an orange juice for my wife please, Alan." I was speechless as Greg guided me to our table and pulled out my chair for me to sit down.

"You may not have alcohol tonight, my love, much as you deserve something a little special. You have to take care of our baby," he said, smiling from ear to ear.

"What baby? What are you talking about?" I said, shaking. Different emotions racing through me; anger at the denial of a sumptuous glass of Pinot was still slightly ahead of disbelief and hope at that moment.

"My darling Caroline, you are pregnant. Doctor Frampton called this afternoon with the news."

"What? But how? How far along, is he sure?"

"Absolutely certain. He was totally baffled and ran the test three times to make sure. We are approximately four weeks along and that is why you have been feeling a little funny. I am so proud of you, Caroline."

He gave me a huge kiss, which under normal circumstances would have made me cringe; in our local pub in front of people, but I was so overwhelmed I didn't resist.

April 7th

I've hardly slept since Greg broke the news, beside myself excited about the prospect of having a baby after all this time trying and also worried it was a mistake, that Dr Frampton will call back to apologise for the mix up. It has finally sunk in that I am pregnant, and last night I slept like a log.

April 12th

Wow I had a vivid dream last night. It may mean nothing, but I guess we will find out at the first scan.

I was sitting at my dressing table, looking into the mirror. There was a glow coming from my chest; it was the necklace Greg bought me in Troutbeck.

I remember thinking, even in my dream, that it wasn't easy for silver to radiate a golden halo. As I stared at the pendant it grew larger and then came alive.

The silver Jill, turned and winked at me with her big brown eyes and two baby rabbits bounced into view.

I awoke with a start and the first thought that popped into my head was, "Oh! It's twins!"

Cows in the Queue

by Rae Magson

About Rae

My interest in the Ashburton Writers' Group goes back many years, and I still love it —meeting new people and listening to their fascinating stories.

I write every day, have a love of words, but the person I most admire is Stephen King, author of many books. Not so much for his plots but how he keeps the action going. He is a master of the writing craft.

I research and write family history mostly, but the following two stories were assignments for the Writers' Group.

Cows in the Queue

There were cows in the queue, two of them, named Letty and Hetty, and they were accompanied by their husband, Bergie the bull. But wait a minute, that was not allowed! Noah had commanded that the animals come in pairs, one male and one female.

Bergman Bartholomew Bull was not happy, not happy at all. He had lots of wives, but these two were his favourites, he could not do without either of them. Ahead of them in the queue were the sheep, behind them were the pigs, two of each; they were conforming to the rules, more fool them.

They proceeded to the entrance. Noah bellowed at Bergie, "One male, one female, didn't you hear?"

Bergie said, "I will not go one step further with my two girls. If you don't let us in, the world will have no cows, and then no milk, no cream, no butter, no cheese, no yoghurt, in fact you won't be able to do without us. I can't choose between these girls, they are both precious to me, as well they are young and fertile, they will have lots of little calves."

Noah pondered on this for minute and then said, "Okay, I will let you in, but you are all to go to your corner, and stay there, no telling anyone else what I have allowed."

Bergie grinned to himself, thought of the parties they would have in their corner, even perhaps rocking the boat, and pitied the next door neighbours; the docile sheep and the pigs. Their main interest though was food, lots and lots of it.

That is the story of why Mid-Canterbury has so many cows. Bergie, Letty and Hetty all did their part. If DNA tests were done on the present-day cows, you would find they are all descended from Bergie and either Letty or Hetty.

The song says, "The Animals went in two by two", but we know better, all the animals went in two by two except for the bull and his two wives.

In this Neighbourhood

by Rae Magson

In this Neighbourhood

As a man just turning sixty-four years of age, I was retiring from my job, and I had so many plans.

They were the usual sort of things—golfing, travelling, going out with the boys sometimes, and walking. Walking you think—why walking?

Well, not in the usual sense. Sometimes I just want to be on my own, so I leave the wife in her room sound asleep. Oh yes, we sleep in different rooms; that has been happening for several years. A mutual decision.

In the middle of the night, I don black clothes, even put a little black on my face, just to make sure I am not easily seen in this neighbourhood. I know the dark streets in town too, so mostly that is where I go. My interest is to look for lights that are on in the houses, so I creep up to the windows, very, very quietly, sometimes hide in the bushes. You would be surprised what I see. Not always females, sometimes I watch two males together, but mostly it is the young women who interest me. They often don't pull the curtains properly; a little crack will do for me to look in and see what they are doing. Little children do not always behave properly, and I make sure I am hidden, as I don't want them to think I am the "boogie man".

One woman in particular interests me. She is mostly alone, and so often she is crying. I would like to go in and comfort her but realise this would be taken the wrong way. But I look in many times. She is so beautiful. I dream about her. Then there was the wintry night, I stood in my usual place looking at her to see what was happening. The door opens and a man comes in. She is obviously terrified of him, and backs into the corner, and says, "No, please don't." He hits her; she falls on the bed, and terrible things start to happen.

What should I do? If I go to try and help her the police will ask why I was there, so what do I do? Yes, I'm a coward. I turn and run home as fast as I can. A few days after I read about a young woman who is missing, and I know deep down that it is her. There is a photo on the television and in the newspaper. There is even a reward. I phone anonymously, and said I had seen a man leaving there, not telling of my looking through a window.

A few days later there was a knock on my door, it was the police wanting to interview me; they had traced my call. That is the reason I am now sitting in a police cell, being charged with murder.

Truly, that is my story, you believe it, don't you?

2021 Paper Plus Short Story Competition Winners

12 to 15 years

The Crack

by Memphis Keen

The Crack

I was out at sea on a cruise ship going to the North Island for a holiday. The sun was going down, so I decided to get some sleep. When I was walking back to my cabin, I saw this crack and I thought my imagination was playing tricks on me. I ignored it and went to sleep.

When I woke up the crack was humongous!!! The sea water was leaking down in the crack. I was freaking out about drowning. I tried to stay calm, but then I burst into a mess. I started saying to myself, "Am I going to die?" Everyone else was distressed too. I looked below the boat.

Suddenly, I felt my stomach turning upside down. Fortunately, it was just water in the crack, so I swam up and out. Sadly, only two people pulled through out of thirty, me and a person called Jeff. He was 25 years old and five years older than me. We were floating on our backs. Although I was exhausted from swimming out of the crack. After what felt like forever, a helicopter finally came.

Jeff and I traveled our separate ways and both got back to our families. I watched the news and the news reporter said, "The crack is getting bigger. Scientists think that we have 48 hours until the earth splits in half from the crack. EVACUATE NOW!"

I listened and fled to England. I got a hotel room and settled in. After forty hours the whole world was shaking. I got a notification on my phone saying, "This is not an earthquake, the earth is splitting." As soon as I read the message, I started falling.

While falling, I looked down. BANG!!! I fell face first. Luckily there was a lot of water half the height of me, and I'm six foot. I was in pain from the fall, so I took my time. Seven minutes later, a light hovered over me, and I could finally see. I looked around and saw cars, bodies, etc. I started walking down the hallway. BANG! Parts of buildings fell right behind me. I had goosebumps all over my body. I walked and eventually I saw a sign saying, 'Welcome to the underworld'. I was thinking, "Is this real?"

A voice said, "Yes, this is real, follow me."

So, I followed him. He was in a dark coat. Then I saw pools, not water pools, lava pools. I realised that e v e r y o n e   t h e r e   w a s   s k e l e t o n s. "AHHHHHHHHHHHHH!!!" I screamed. I started to run back down the long and dark hall. I tripped and passed out. When I woke up, I was hanging upside down above a lava pit ready to be dropped. I looked to my side, and I saw a lot of skeletons about to lower me. The man said, "Don't trust strangers, bye." I fell into the lava.

I woke up in a sweat. Oh, was it a nightmare? Wait, I'm on a boat right now.

Life in the Trenches

by Kate Rickard

Life in the Trenches

21/7/1917

Dear diary,

Death, my mind is filled with death. Gunshots, blood, screams and shouts. Diary, why am I here? I have a life to live. If I stay here, I will die.

The conditions are horrendous. Many of the lads here have severe trench foot, with pus oozing through their thick leather boots.

Will that be my ending? Or will I be shot to the ground and left to struggle and die in pain? Left to rot and smell like those already fallen?

I am more depressed since I last wrote, as food is sparse, water gone. The sun has left the sky. It has given up on trying to brighten the days, instead gun smoke fills the large expanse of air. All the lads I used to chat with have fallen, lying still in awkward positions on the trench floor around us.

My hands are covered in blood of those I do not know. I am now used to the gruesome feeling of standing on bodies as we march on formally toward our destination, and am fine with the stench of death that before made me vomit.

As I write this, I am watching vermin eat my old friend Peter, who fell two weeks ago, lapping up every trickle of blood and savouring his maggot infested tongue as it holds it up between its small paws. I watch as its stomach grows bigger. Until it runs away, face bright and cheery.

I am on rest now and am supposed to be sleeping, but how when I am watching lives be lost by the second? Tommy, my comrade, has now fallen, his fresh lifeless body lying limp on top of Peter. His nerves still twitching, making him move in ways unimaginable.

God, is this really your will?

Please, God, save our souls.

My Mysterious Encounter

by Niamh Hawe

My Mysterious Encounter

What I thought was going to be just a normal, relaxing day turned out to be so much more; it was a day I will never forget!

It started out quite normally. I snoozed my alarm at least twice but eventually the sharp, high-pitched bark of my Border Collie puppy, Luna, denied me any more sleep. Sitting impatiently at the foot of my bed, she was barking, desperately trying to wake me. Her lead on the floor next to her was a not-so-subtle hint that she wanted to go for a jog. How could I resist that little furry black and white face staring up at me with her huge, brown puppy eyes?

As much as Luna wanted to go, I just had to have my morning coffee before we went. The luscious aroma drifted to my nose as I gave Luna a few treats and then finally sat down to sip my morning brew and read the news. I was scrolling through Stuff, and I saw three articles that caught my attention – one about a car crash, one about more Covid cases, and one about another mysterious black panther sighting. After reading the first two articles I felt sad and devastated that Covid was still in the country, but the last article intrigued me. Being a vet meant I got very curious about anything to do with animals – especially puzzling ones. A panther in New Zealand? "Let's go, Luna," I called, and she ran to the door, her tail wagging frantically.

As we headed outside, the cool breeze hit me straight in the face and reminded me it was now Autumn. I attached Luna to her lead, put in my AirPods and off we jogged. Living on the outskirts of town meant we had lots of forest, parks and tracks nearby that we liked to run through. Today we chose a path through the forest because soon it would be too damp and cold to run there. After a while we stopped and sat down on a bench for a quick drink and energy reboot.

It wasn't that long after our short break, when all of a sudden, Luna sprinted around me in circles and finally stopped, hiding behind my legs. Her lead was wrapped so tightly around me that I fell to my knees on the rocky path. She was frightened, but of what? I didn't have a clue.

I felt like someone was watching me, and as I lifted my head I froze as my eyes met two beady, big, hazel-green eyes staring directly at me from amongst the shrubbery on the forest floor. With a body too big to be a cat, a tail too long to be a dog, and fur too black to be a tiger, it hit me that I was looking back at my reflection in the mysterious black panther's eyes!

And that's How the Fight Started...

By Deborah Carter

About Deborah

Deborah Carter was born in the UK and moved to New Zealand as a child.

She is a wife, mother to five beautiful daughters and grandmother to seven.

Works full time but spends her limited free time reading and writing.

Deborah has been a member of the Ashburton Writers Group for sixteen years and has self-published five books.

Website: www.deborahcarterauthor.com

Instagram: @debbiecarter27

Facebook: @debbiecarter27

And that's How the Fight Started...

"..and that's how the fight started, Officer." The young woman dressed in a floral bathrobe and handcuffs, fluttered long blackened lashes at the large man in uniform.

The man on the gurney choked out, "And that's how the fight started? You've got to be fuckin' kiddin' me." The officer turned to the deathly pale man with his pen held at the ready and nodded for him to continue. "The Christmas party was a bust except for dancing with this little vixen, and so, when she suggested we take the, um, 'dancing' back to her place, I was eager to follow. On arrival, I was momentarily stunned by the abnormal amount of Christmas decorations littering her apartment, but as she tugged at my belt, the blood in my brain moved heads and thought wasn't an option. Naked, our bodies continued the dance, horizontally this time. She felt so good, and as I reared back ready for the gravy stroke, she suddenly screamed "not the tree" and I froze with my hips pulled back, bum in the air, and then I felt an unbearable burn lance through my body by way of my arse. It seared my rear, radiating, magnifying and naturally to escape the pain I thrust forward. Big mistake! On re-entry, the friction and her immense grip, had my control spiralling, and I screamed out my orgasm, my cock pulsed and every muscle clenched, including my arse muscles. The foreign object, still inserted, cracked under the pressure, and then I didn't know what threshold I was jetting through; pain, pleasure, pleasure, pain.

Moments later, I was dragged away from her, still seeing a haze of red, and then these two started screaming at each other. Still naked, she attacked my molester with a large gift-wrapped box, complete with red bow and smashed him repeatedly with it until the sirens overtook all other sound and the door burst open, and the rest you know." He drew a shuddering breath as yet another shard of glass was plucked from his anus with a pair of tweezers. "I think the shot you gave me is wearing off," he said to the nurse.

The officer turned to the other man sitting beside the gurney; a different nurse attending the gash across his eyebrow with a needle and thread. "Is this how the fight started?" he asked.

The man nodded and flinched. "Pretty much. I saw my girlfriend leaving the party with this dude and followed them back to her place. When I let myself in the door, I discovered them locked in a sweaty embrace and saw red. I grabbed the stupid glass Christmas decoration and stuck it where the sun don't shine, sorry dude," he said, looking at the man on the cot, "but you were bangin' my girl."

All eyes turned to the woman, and her shoulders hunched right up to her ears before dropping again. "It's Christmas," she said, as if that would explain everything. Everyone stared in disbelief as she turned to her boyfriend. "Ask him his name," she said. He turned toward the man and raised his eyes in question.

"Cringle, Christopher Cringle," the man replied. He frowned, as if trying to work out why that would explain anything."

The woman grinned as her boyfriend's frown disappeared and a quiet "oh" left his lips as he understood.

The officer cleared his throat. "Let me get this straight. Your neighbour called, reporting a domestic; we arrive to find your girlfriend beating the crap out of you with a box because you molested Mr. Cringle with a glass Christmas tree for banging your girlfriend, and the reason she was banging him is 'because it's Christmas?"

The boyfriend looked slightly abashed as he said "Yeah, that's about it, Officer. But hearing his name explains everything. Because simply put, I know she'll DO anything Christmassy."

Santa

By Deborah Carter

Santa

Santa's feet are in the hearth, with his sugar plums in sight

Our Rottweiler, Dex, licks his chops, just hankering for a bite

I left a note of warning, upon the chimney pot

I guess Santa never read it, and now he's in a spot.

He deserves a little discomfort; I feel it's kind of fair

After the mess he left here last year, size 12 footprints on the stair

Mum thought that I'd been messy, and punished me for the crime

It didn't matter that I pointed out; my shoe is just size nine.

Now Santa's knees are shaking, his fear is palpable

Wondering if I'll help him, or let my dog chomp on his ball

I note I'm on the nice list and make my mind up in a hurry

Pushing past my puppy, and to Santa I do scurry

Come on Santa, bend your knees, I'll help you from the hearth

The tree's just there, the lights all lit, see, I've cleared a path

One, two three, four gifts, "Is that all I get?" I hissed

"I just saved your bollocks!" I was well and truly pissed.

He turned around and eyed my dog and then gave me a glare

Held his empty sack up, to show nothing else was there

Disappointment filled my body, and my stomach hit the floor

And Santa took advantage and scuttled toward the door

"Um, I don't think so, Santa, that's not how you came in"

Dex sidling past to guard the door makes me want to grin

"Up the chimney, Santa. With tradition we must uphold

So, step on up and touch your nose, if you'd be so bold"

With a shake of his head, he walks to me and tugs his beard down

"It's me, your dad, not Santa Clause." My brows turn to a frown

He whispers, "Santa isn't real, luv. I dress up, it's all a ruse

"So they were your size 12 last year I got blamed for," I accuse.

His mouth turned down and his head drooped low as he shook it back and forth

"You've seen my shoes, they are size 10." Now that gave me a pause

If it wasn't him and it wasn't me, then who came to our house that day?

A jangling sound came from the roof, "could that be Santa's sleigh?"

Dad grabbed me quick, and sofa dived, and covered us with a rug

Santa slithered down to the hearth, and gave his sack a tug

It landed with a heavy thump as it hit the wooden floor

And we watched as Santa darted round, and checked behind the door

Satisfied he'd not been heard, he tipped his heavy sack

One by one, gaily wrapped, each present neatly stacked

Job well done, he ate the cookie and took a swig of drink

His roving eye ran round the room, and I swear he gave a wink

Had we been found I wondered, as Dad held me firmly in place

To be caught spying on Santa Clause, would be a big disgrace

he rumbled, as he turned without a care

And for a man so heavy, he fare pelted up those stairs

We didn't move a muscle; we just waited one minute, two

And Santa could be heard above, as he finished and flushed the loo

Then back he came to collect his sack and into the hearth he bent

With a loud he touched his nose and up the chimney he went

Dad stood slowly, his mouth agape and turned an eye to me

But I was busy looking at the mass of gifts beneath our tree

"He's real," I said, "Can you believe it? I turned toward my dad

And for the first time, this whole year, his face, it wasn't sad

He entered the hall and stared at the steps, a size 12 footprint or two are there

Like the one that had been there a year ago, the same print upon the stair

So much fighting and accusations it caused, it was still an open case

Now his eyes are bright with unshed tears, but a smile lights up his face

"Get to bed and take Dex too; it's time that you were sleeping"
He followed me up, and then peeled off, to the room where Mum lay weeping
He told her the story, and relayed all his worries, shared with her his fear
Then he pulled her in and hugged her tight, and wiped away a tear

Christmas morning came and went, unwrapped gifts, and all well fed
Darkness came, the child's asleep, and the adults fell into bed
As they made love she chuckled with mirth, as the story she recalls
How her husband as Santa got stuck in the hearth, and Dex nearly chewed off his balls

Handle with Care

By Deborah Carter

Handle with Care

The gold filling glinted as the dark, heavy-set man smiled. He grasped the slender, pale hand of his daughter where it lay, skin almost translucent against the shining, black material of his suit.

Annabella walked softly, her feet barely kissing the floorboards. She held herself erect, a floating statue, as the white, high-necked gown shrouded her body, her flawless face of porcelain skin, naked of paints and powders except for her lips where a touch of gloss shone.

She wouldn't look at him or me either as they drew close. "Handle with care," his voice rumbled, his eyes filled with the hatred I'd come to expect. A smirk on his cruel, thin lips, the barely veiled threat unmistakable, as he gave his daughters hand to me, the passing of a rare possession. And how true that was.

Rare indeed! She was stunning; a maiden, young and innocent, but a possession none the less. And now she was mine!

I'd waited seemingly forever for the moment I would receive this gift. This payment? An agreement fulfilled as was promised since her birth. Finally, standing within the same space as this sixteen-year-old woman-child was an almost ethereal experience, her very essence seemingly transporting itself from where her hand touched mine.

I barely held myself together long enough to say, 'I do' and to hear her softly whispered acceptance of our vows. The need rising, surging to claim that which now belonged to me—the innocence which I now owned. The body I would devour, as lust grew hot and heavy in my loins, I would destroy her and enjoy every second of it. Her white skin would flush pink as I take her over and over, and then turn red by my hand. Just as my mother's had before Annabella's father killed her. Annabella may be her father's little princess, but now she is my wife, and her life is in my hands.

Handle with care, hah! If that old bastard thinks he can dictate how I should treat his precious child, he can go fuck himself.

The preacher drawled out the final readings, the prayer and then came the words, "I now pronounce you husband and wife, you may kiss your bride." The smile I gave her was cold, calculating, and I expected her to turn and run back to Daddy. She surprised me by shuffling a step closer, splaying her pale, slender fingers, nails tipped red like blood, against my black jacket. She rose on tiptoe, bringing her face level with my chin and tilted her head back, poised, statuesque, waiting for me to close the void and taste her lips. What trickery was this? Our eyes met; I expected a timid, frightened child, sobbing as she clung to her daddy's arm, begging him to save her from me, the beast, but she looked at me as though I were her hero. She would learn soon enough.

Annabella offered her lips, and who was I to refuse? Two could play this game. I snared her hand beneath mine, leant in and barely touched my lips to hers. We turned and made our way down the aisle, the family's hatred on either side palpable. The look on her father's face should have forewarned me; something was afoot. What was the betting the old prick had locked a chastity belt on his child? Anything to stop me from defiling her. Like that would stop me.

Marching us directly to the brides ready-room, I stood her in the centre of the floor, walked around her as though sizing up a prized heifer and commanded, "Strip!"

She offered me a gentle smile; that was her only movement.

"I'm not your father, Annabella, I will not treat you with kid gloves, I take what I want. My treatment of you will be the complete opposite of his, people call me 'the beast' for good reason." I waited for her to cower, for the tears to slide, but all I received was an even bigger smile, and those expressive eyes gazed at me with hero worship.

Grabbing her gown, I tore it from her slender form and let my gaze travel her naked body. I couldn't suppress the gasp of surprise as my hands reached, fingertips grazing over her skin, gently stroking along her shoulders, down her arms, across her breasts, her nipples pebbling as I passed them. A tear escaped, sliding down her cheek and dripping on my hand. I spun her carefully, palms travelling her spine as she glanced over her shoulder at me.

Shaking my head in disbelief, I knew I would stay true to my word 'that I would be her father's complete opposite; this poor child had known nothing but pain. I may be a beast, but her father was the monster. As I ran my hands over the old, leathered ridges of scar tissue, soothed over the newer barely healing welts and stared at her rainbowed skin, purple, yellow, and green I vowed to myself, this possession, I would indeed, handle with care.

The Recipe

By Deborah Carter

The Recipe

"Drive!" I ordered as I threw open the passenger door and, hauling Jonah across my body, thrust his torso and head toward the tarmac which blurred beneath the speeding car. Jonah screamed, "Don't, God don't, no aagh." His voice changed to an agonized shriek as I held him down and the road became painted with chunks of flesh and blood.

Don't judge me for my actions. Yes, I could have put a bullet in his head, but that would have been far too kind. I'd promised he would pay, that he'd suffer as he'd made her suffer. And I never go back on my word.

I closed the book and glanced around the room; some of the faces were a slight shade of grey.

"Thank you all for coming to the launch of my latest novel. The floor is now open for questions."

One man stood, shuffling his feet a little, uncomfortable at being first.

"How do you create a story like this?" he asked.

"Well," I say, "it's not as difficult as one would think. Scribble down a few words, an idea forms, add a handful of characters, throw in some description, to colour, flavour the story. A pinch of romance to tug at the heartstrings, a big dollop of heroism, (everyone likes a hero) and then work it, reword, rewrite, over and over. Mixing, adjusting, adding a touch of spice here and there. Once it gels, let it rest, while you work on final touches, the icing on the cake so to speak. The cover and blurb. After all, if you see a mushed up, messy cake that's not appetising to the eye, you wouldn't purchase it."

"So, you're telling us, that to write a story is like baking a cake?" a voice from the back of the room called out.

"Raise your hands if, as a child, you made mudpies, patting the gloopy, sticky dirt into baking bowls."

The room was suddenly filled with waving hands.

"Now, how many of you were disappointed with the bland, black mess, and added bits of grass, plucked flowers from your parents' flowerbeds to decorate, to beautify, to bring your product to life?"

The waving hands raised again.

"See, even as a child, you were creating, using your imaginations.

Everything in life is a recipe. We are given a blueprint; birth, school, work, die. It's the individual's choice as to what ingredients are added. What colours are preferred, how emotions and actions mould your creation, bake and decorate, and they've just written the story of their life.

That's how I create my novels."

"Next question please!"

And then the Car Broke Down

By Deirdre Moses

About Deirdre

Deirdre Moses has always enjoyed writing. Even as a child, her teacher used to leave reading her stories until last as she felt they were always a treat.

Over the years, Deirdre has written freelance articles for several publications, has self-published two children's books, and joined Ashburton Writers Group in 2018.

She now writes for a local magazine and has a slot on local radio to read her poems. Deirdre thoroughly enjoys the camaraderie of Writers Group. She enjoys the challenge of the monthly assignments and hearing the fellow members share theirs. She will be looking at publishing more of her adult-themed short stories and poems in the near future.

And then the Car Broke Down

Chloe got in the car and slammed the door. The seat belt kept jamming as she yanked on it with anger. Michael climbed into the driver's seat and gripped the steering wheel for a moment. Chloe was quiet as she wasn't sure if his angry outburst was over or whether it would continue. Much to her surprise, he threw back his head and laughed. "Taught that bitch a lesson!" he shouted triumphantly as Chloe stared at him, open mouthed.

"How the hell was making that poor girl cry, getting us kicked out of the restaurant and barred for life teaching her a lesson?!" she asked incredulously.

"Well they advertised that your first drink was free if you dined there. So, I wanted a double rum and coke." Michael replied with a sneer.

"But it clearly stated it was only tap beer or house wine!" Chloe countered. "Did you really not see the sign?"

"Got my free rum and coke though!" He laughed. "You have to be as intimidating as possible to get a freebie. My mates and I do it all the time."

He chuckled away to himself. "I could never afford to eat at a place like that, bloody rip off. There's a really posh restaurant around the corner. Shall we see what we can get from there? We'll see if we can get the actual meal this time."

Chloe just stared at him and shook her head. This was her first dating experience and one she would never forget, for all the wrong reasons. Michael seemed so lovely when they chatted online. He offered no clue that he was a cheapskate and absolute bully.

She was silently chiding her friends for insisting it was time for her get on with her life. Her husband Steve had passed away four years ago, and they had been together since high school.

"Please just take me home," Chloe said to her date.

Michael looked delighted. "Sure thing, babe," he said and winked at her suggestively. He reached over and put his hand on her knee.

She swatted his hand away with disgust. "No, Michael, this date is over! I cannot comprehend that you offered to take me to a lovely restaurant that you couldn't even afford, just so you could make a scene! This is a game to you?" Her voice was rising now, and her cheeks were flushed with anger and humiliation. "You find it funny to belittle people, humiliate me and completely embarrass all the staff in front of the other guests?! Just take me home!"

Michael looked shocked. "How dare you!" His expression suddenly changed, and his eyes grew dark with rage. "You ungrateful bitch! You came out expecting a free meal, and that's what I was going to get for you!"

Chloe immediately realised she had made a mistake when agreeing to allow Michael to pick her up from her home. Now he knew where she lived, and she suspected he was going to prove difficult when they got back there.

Then the car broke down. It suddenly completely died, and Michael managed to steer it to the side of the road as it coasted and came to a complete stop.

"Dammit!" he screamed and smacked the steering wheel. "Useless bloody piece of shit!" Chloe was frightened now. Things had escalated massively and now she was stuck with this sociopath.

With all the calmness she could muster, she discretely sent a text to Uber for immediate pick up. She noted the street signs and hurriedly sent them directions. Michael didn't even notice. By this stage he was outside kicking the tyres on the car and slamming his fist into the bonnet. He was ranting to himself and had completely succumbed to the rage that had consumed him.

Chloe sat in the car. She looked hopefully at every pair of headlights that approached them, willing it to be her ride, but then slumped in defeat as they continued past.

Michael had stormed off down the roadside, screaming in absolute fury about the useless piece of shit vehicle and the stupid ungrateful bitch who ruined his night and cost him a free meal.

After what seemed an eternity, a car slowed and pulled up behind Chloe, and she rushed out towards it. Michael was now storming towards the Uber vehicle, spitting with anger and screaming at her. "What the hell do you think you're doing?! This is all your fault."

Chloe quickly locked the passenger door. She shouted, "Get me out of here!" to the alarmed driver.

Without hesitation, the driver took off, spinning the wheels in the shingle as he did so. She watched in her side mirror as her enraged date stood screaming and ranting and thumping the roof of his car.

Chloe took a deep breath and quietly deleted Tinder from her phone.

Fairy Tale Remix

By Deirdre Moses

Fairy Tale Remix

It was a beautiful summer's day, and a group of friends had decided to have a picnic at their favourite spot in the nearby forest. They had all brought their own cushions and individually packed lunches to ensure they could still meet whilst following the social distancing rules.

As they were setting up, a rabbit came bounding up to the group at lightning speed. He was so transfixed on his pocket watch, he wasn't looking where he was going and bounced straight into Little Red Riding Hood! They both tumbled over, and the poor rabbit landed face first in Red Riding Hood's cupcakes.

"Oh dear! Oh dear! I'm awfully sorry, miss, but I'm late! I'm so very late!" Rabbit apologised as he tried to wipe the frosting from his face with a large checkered handkerchief.

"Watch where you're going next time!" scolded Red Riding Hood. "Where on earth are you rushing to that's so important you had to ruin my lunch?"

"I beg your pardon, Ma'am," Rabbit replied. "I'm on a very important mission for Alice. She has just collected enough stickers from New World to get the final knife for her collection, and the promotion ends today!"

The entire group of friends let out a collective gasp. "So today is the last day?!" Cinderella asked in a panicked voice. The friends all began hurriedly packing up their things.

"Dammit, I've only got enough stickers for one knife!" complained Snow White. Similar comments and mutterings spread throughout the group.

"So you see!" continued Rabbit, "I simply must get there before they close, or heaven forbid, run out!"

The group nodded in agreement.

"How on earth did Alice manage to spend enough on groceries to get the whole set?" asked Snow White. "Don't you have to spend seven thousand dollars to earn that three dollar knife? What the heck did she spend all that money on?"

Rabbit rolled his eyes and replied, "Toilet paper, of course!"

Rabbit checked his pocket watch again. "Oh dear! I'm so late!" and with that he scampered off down the path towards town.

Papa Bear had been quietly observing this exchange between his friends and shook his head. "Stupid humans," he whispered under his breath at the absurdity of it all.

Baby Bear was completely confused. "Why don't they just shit in the woods like us, Dad?"

Mama Bear beamed proudly at Baby Bear. "Good question, dear boy. As you've just learnt, humans have an awful lot of evolving to do before they're as clever as us."

Suddenly a muffled voice, seemingly coming from under a rock, said, "I have an idea!" The bewildered friends looked all around, trying to see who had spoken.

"It's me, Mr. Tortoise!" the voice replied as his head and limbs slowly appeared from his shell.

"Oh dear!" Cinderella giggled. "I thought you were a very pretty rock and nearly sat on you!"

"Now that would've made my day." The dirty minded old Tortoise grinned. Cinderella blushed.

"I wish I had seen that!" piped up Pinocchio. "Oooops, um, sorry, Cinderella. I've just always fancied you and I didn't mean to say that out loud!"

Cinderella glared at Pinocchio. He hung his head and shifted awkwardly as he realised it wasn't his nose that was growing.

Snow White broke the silence and rapidly changed the subject. "Well, Mr. Tortoise, we would love to hear your idea, but I'm worried that because we didn't know you were here, we are now over the limit of how many are allowed to congregate at once!"

Mr. Tortoise chuckled. "Well, my dear, technically I am actually isolating at home."

The friends all laughed. "Of course you are!" said Snow White.

"I've been patiently waiting for Sleeping Beauty to wake. She's asleep in a hammock deep in the forest. I've been waiting for years. Thankfully I'm in no hurry and I have the time."

"Wait, what?!" gasped Snow White.

Everyone turned to look at Prince Charming. "Did you know about this?" Snow White asked him.

Prince Charming replied, "Of course I knew where Sleeping Beauty was. There's no way in hell I'm kissing her until her test results come back negative!"

The friends all nodded in agreement.

"As I was saying," said Tortoise, "I have an idea. As none of you have enough stickers for your free knives, how about you combine all your stickers, and you may just have enough between you to get the full set."

Prince Charming drew his sword. "Good idea, old chap, I'll be ready to put up a fight with you all to gain ownership of the knife set. It seems the obvious and fair solution."

"No, no, no," chuckled the old Tortoise. "We sell the knives on Trademe and split the profit."

"Wait!" said Red Riding Hood as she checked her phone.

"I've just seen on Facebook that New World has run out of knives!"

"NNNOOOOOO!" the others cried.

The humans all slumped back down on their cushions, defeated and devastated. They decided to break the social distancing rules in order to comfort each other. They all sat in a close circle, held hands and observed a minute's silence to mourn their loss.

The three bears looked at each other and shook their heads. "Stupid humans," said Baby Bear as he gleefully stole all their lunches.

Getting Muddy

By Deirdre Moses

Getting Muddy

The day was warm after days of rain, so I got out in the sun

It was so very overdue, the gardening had begun.

In my shorts and T-shirt, I delighted in my flowers

I grabbed my tools and gardening gloves; I'd be out here for hours.

With the gentle rustling of the leaves, and bird song from above

The gorgeous sunshine on my back, I then removed my gloves.

I felt the mud beneath my touch, and marvelled in its texture

I thought connection with the earth was an added extra.

As I knelt in my flowerbed, my endorphins were releasing

My joy at being one with the earth meant my happiness was increasing.

I decided to lose a layer, off with shorts and top

I felt the sun upon my skin so then I shed the lot

So here I was stark naked now, as mother earth intended

Hoping the neighbours wouldn't see, lest they be offended.

I felt the mud between my toes, the feeling was delightful!

This sudden thought to garden nude was really quite insightful.

So I got right in amongst it, I knelt, then sat, then rolled

Mud was where it had never been, quite the sight to behold!

So I pulled some weeds and revelled in, the dirt under my nails

I enjoyed that time with mother earth, the insects, slugs and snails.

After many enjoyable hours my hubby arrived home

The sight that lay before him – he was completely thrown!

Stark naked, rolling in the mud – a sight he'd never seen.

That naked day with mother earth, the happiest I'd ever been.

2021 Paper Plus Short Story Competition Winners

Adult
(16 years and over)

The Last Laugh

by Adrienne Moody

The Last Laugh

1899 – Clara hefted the heavy kettle from the coal range and emptied hot water into the bucket. Although slight for her fourteen years, she was no stranger to hard work. The oldest in a family with six children, she had always helped to clean, cook and care for the younger ones. Then, eighteen months ago her mother had given birth once again. The midwife came early in the morning and, by noon, a pale, wizened baby had arrived on this earth, decided that life wasn't worth the effort and departed. Clara's Mother haemorrhaged. The doctor was summoned but arrived too late to be of any assistance.

The family struggled along for twelve months with Clara working from dawn until well past dusk. Then one day their father took the horse and gig into town and came home with the news that Aunty Ethel was to become their stepmother.

Clara found it difficult to adjust. When a neighbour heard that a retired sea captain was looking for a housekeeper, she applied for the position. In spite of her youth, she was deemed to be suitable.

At first all was well. The captain was taciturn and often gloomy, but he left her to get on with her work. Clara soon had the little cottage gleaming, and she often sang as she went about her tasks. With better food and an easier life her skinny body rounded out a little.

Then came the night when the captain came to her little room off the kitchen just before she fell asleep. At first it only happened occasionally but then more regularly.

Clara mulled over the problem as she scrubbed the floors. She had no money and, without references, might not find another job. How could she put a stop to the unwelcome nocturnal visits?

2019 – Lisa put down her coffee mug and sank into a chair on the verandah. The night was still warm, and she could see a glimpse of the sun's last rays shining on the estuary. Peace at last. Her two boys were asleep. The furniture was all in place, and she just had a few boxes left to sort.

Idly she let her mind wander over the last few years. She had married young. Tony had burst into her life just as she started her training as an early childhood teacher. Soon they had plans – a house of their own, travel, children … Then the children came along rather earlier than intended. The house had to be put on hold, but they rented a small flat. Tony worked in an office. He had a gift for talking to people and soon charmed his way to promotion. After Josh was born, they became a real little family. Picnics on the beach on Saturday, long lazy Sundays.

Ben arrived three years later. He wasn't such an easy baby, and Lisa had started to work on her early childhood training again. Life seemed to be a continual round of housework, childcare and study. Tony was working hard too. Often, he stayed at the office in the evening to finish some paperwork, although it made no difference to his salary. She believed him when he explained that it was all about getting a better job. Even when she found a receipt in his pocket for one of the city's most expensive restaurants. The sort of place they never went to because they were still saving for that house deposit. Even when one of his co-workers mentioned to her quietly that she should watch out for the glamorous secretary. She laughed it off. Not Tony. She trusted her husband. Until the night that he told her he was going to a conference in Rotorua. His car hit a logging truck and he was killed instantly. The secretary survived, although she was left with a permanent scar on one perfect cheek. There was no conference. Just a booking at a seedy little motel.

The days after the accident passed in a blur of grief, until the evening when she sat down to work out their finances. The house deposit account hadn't grown quite as much as she expected. Tony had always taken care of the bills and the bank statements. Auckland real estate was on a roll, sweeping rental prices along with it. Even their little flat wasn't affordable any longer – not on a benefit.

When a friend rang to invite her and the boys along on a trip to the beach, she thought it might cheer her up. And it did. As they left the city behind, she felt herself relax. But the real bonus came as they drove home with sun-warmed, sandy children nearly asleep in the back seat. They drove past a rundown cottage on the edge of a country town. And the sign on the gate said 'for rent'.

Three weeks later, here they were. It wasn't a palace, but the rent was manageable. Behind her she heard a strange noise. It sounded as if something was being dragged over the floorboards. A quick search didn't show any obvious cause. Perhaps it was just the way the wind blew in through the back porch.

The next weeks were happy ones. Josh liked his new school. Ben's pre-school said they could offer her a few hours work occasionally. The cottage creaked at night and the wind moaned through the trees outside. Sometimes a bird gave a strange, high-pitched cry. All a part of getting used to life away from the city.

On a trip to the little public library one day, Lisa stopped to look at a display featuring photos of local houses. Her cottage was amongst them. Underneath copies of very old newspaper articles told a little of its history.

The Sun – 30th November 1899 – Sea Captain and Maid Both Missing

Rev. Thomas Cameron called at Captain Smyth's home yesterday on church business. He found the back door ajar, but no-one appeared to be at home. The hens were still shut up in the henhouse for the night although it was 10:30 in the morning. Thinking this odd, he investigated further. He found the furniture disturbed in the kitchen and a blood stain on the floor. At this stage the Rev. Cameron alerted a neighbour who called in the local constabulary.

Further articles detailed the story that shook the little community for months. The captain was described as a fine, upstanding gentleman, if a little disinclined to join in conversation. The maid was hardworking, with a pretty singing voice and, when decorum allowed, laughter that pealed like a bell. The local blacksmith was asked to break the lock on a heavy chest where the captain was known to store money and valuables. He always wore the key on a cord around his neck. Very little was found in the chest, leading to speculation that both the cottage's inhabitants had been murdered during a robbery. Eventually the captain's rowing boat was found drifting near the opposite bank of the estuary, but the mystery was never solved.

2019 – As Lisa walked home, she thought about the odd noises that seemed to be a part of her home. Was it the little maid seeking revenge for her murder? Of course it wasn't.

She decided to use the rest of the day to dig over a patch of ground ready to plant vegetables. Once she cleared the weeds the ground wasn't difficult to dig. Perhaps it had been used as a garden before. Her spade hit something hard. She dug deeper and unearthed a bone. Then more bones. Too big for a dog. Perhaps a beloved horse? She phoned the local policeman.

Within an hour or two her backyard was swarming with police. They took the bones away for analysis, along with the pieces that remained from an ancient knife. The verdict was a surprise. Just one skeleton. A tall man, probably buried more than 100 years ago.

One evening a month later, Lisa stood beside her vegetable garden. As the sun slipped behind the hills, she felt an eerie presence. Then laughter that pealed like a bell.

I Am So Cold

by Nigel Dean

About Nigel

Originally from England, my family sailed to New Zealand when I was only eighteen months old.

I enjoyed a career as a Pharmacist and have lived in Ashburton since 1979 with my wife Christine. We have children and grandchildren in Melbourne, Amsterdam and Washington DC.

I have always had an interest in writing and did a Creative Writing course about ten years ago. A busy life since has meant that I have had little opportunity to pursue it further.

Now I have more free time, I entered the following story into the 2021 writers' competition. I have since joined the Ashburton Writers Group. And this is a chance to really work on the creative side of writing.

I Am So Cold

"I am cold, so cold," I cried. "I can't feel my fingers or my toes."

There we were, Jules and me, in real trouble near the summit of Mt Aoraki.

We had met at Everest Inn (near the Everest Base Camp) where I had been working as a chef. Jules was on his way to climb Mt Everest and had stopped for the night. On discovering we both came from the same small town in New Zealand, we agreed to go adventuring together when we got back home.

That was five years ago. Since then, we had spent a good deal of our leisure, climbing and exploring New Zealand. He was rugged and strong, man of few words, but could he climb. It didn't seem to matter to him that the rocks were vertical, covered in scree or ice, he just carried on with little me following along.

Our relationship was totally about adventure and nothing more was ever ventured from either of us. I know I was supposed to be concentrating on the climbing but often I found myself admiring those tree trunks of legs as they conquered everything in front of them.

Sure, I had my uses – I am a dab hand of producing meals from nothing. Give Jules a packet of dry noodles and his response was to open the packet and eat them as they were. After our first trip it was always me who prepared the food, while he set up the campsite – whether it was halfway up a mountain or in a remote bush track.

Initially I was hesitant at times, but as time had gone on, with Jules' tutelage, I had gained a lot more confidence. I knew though that this was the most challenging so far.

As always, Jules had researched well before we left. The weather forecast was fine for the next few days with mild late Spring temperatures. We left the hut at 2a.m. for our anticipated sixteen-hour day.

The climb up went well. Once we reached the snow we roped together. I felt safe knowing that Jules, in front, would hold me, as using our ice axes we scrambled our way upwards. After a very solid slog we eventually reached the summit a little before midday. It was a quiet day on the mountain, and we only saw another two groups of climbers. It really felt as though we were alone in the world.

To say that standing at the summit was a magnificent experience would be an understatement. The view of the lower peaks and glaciers was awesome. I stood there for a few moments just soaking in the scenery. We took photos of the views and each other – a moment never to forget!

We started the climb down and made good progress until we had to negotiate around a bluff. As we moved into a shaded spot, Jules realised his mistake.

"This is too icy to be safe – we must shuffle back."

I saw the look of horror on his face as he started to slide. Even his crampons wouldn't hold, and he slipped on to his back. His axe hit an exposed rock and flew out of his hand. Being much lighter and roped meant I went with him.

"Maggie, grab anything you can," Jules shouted at me. I tried, but there was nothing at all to hold on to, and we started to slide faster and faster down the mountain. I could see the crevasse ahead of us and Jules trying to steer our slide away from it. If anyone could do it, he could. He almost succeeded, but the pace was too fast. With a sickening thud we hit the edge of the crevasse and bounced our way down.

I bumped my head several times and heard a loud crack in my left leg. I felt a searing pain course through my body. We hit the bottom of the crevasse, and as blackness descended, I tried desperately to look for Jules. I saw his limp body a couple of metres away.

I don't know how long it was before I regained some consciousness. Despite all my warm clothes, I don't think I have ever been colder. I tried to move but pain stopped me. I looked toward my leg and cried out in agony as I heard the bones grinding together. I looked towards where I had seen Jules and saw that he was still in the same position. He wasn't moving.

I started to cry. I wasn't ready to die, and I had lost one of the best friends I could ever have hoped to have. Tall and strong and a perfect gentleman. I wished sometimes he had been a bit less of a gentleman, but now I would never know.

I somehow crawled over to his body and held him in my arms. He was so cold, and there was no sign of life. There was nothing I could do but hold him until I died too. Even though we had left our climbing intentions at the hut this morning, by the time anyone realised we were missing it would be far too late.

I drifted into unconsciousness again – my last thought being would I ever wake up again? I was hallucinating in and out of consciousness and was quite sure I saw Jules kneeling beside me holding my shoulders. It couldn't be real, as dead bodies don't do that.

"Wake up, wake up," this illusion was shouting at me, but his voice sounded as though it was coming through a fog. I couldn't understand why I was being shaken. Don't tell me there was an earthquake – it must be a strong one the way I was being shaken around.

"I am cold, so cold," I cried. "I can't feel my fingers or my toes."

"I will keep you warm," that strange disconnected voice again.

"I love you," I cried out. "Why are you dead? I want you; I want you; and I will never have you."

I must have lapsed into unconsciousness again as the next thing I remember was waking up again and being quite sure that Jules was lying beside me with his arms around me. I felt a hardness against me. I reached out and somehow through the fog in my head managed to remove enough of my clothes for him to get inside me. We moved together in that bed of snow, and despite the agonising pain from my leg, I groaned in ecstasy as I felt the warmth flow into me.

As the night continued, I kept coming in and out of consciousness. Every time I came to, I had that same sensation of making love. I couldn't understand what was happening as it wasn't Jules usual voice I could hear – just that strange voice saying, "I love you and never told you. And now it's too late."

How I survived that night I will never know. Many hours later I was vaguely aware of a helicopter hovering above me and shortly after strong arms placing me in the winch and being lifted to safety.

As I was being lifted, I heard the rescuer saying, "That's a nasty break she has and it will be months before she is back on her feet." He continued, "Her partner must have been a goner from the fall looking at those head injuries." I looked down to check if my modesty was intact. To my relief, but also disappointment, it was. I also saw Jules's lifeless body lying in exactly the same place I had first seen him after the fall. All that I thought had happened must have been a hallucination due to the shock I was in. I cried and cried all the way to the hospital and for days afterwards.

It was a major compound fracture, and I was in hospital for many weeks' treatment, for three surgeries, treatment for a severe infection and extensive rehabilitation. Even now I walk with a limp, and apart from a little gentle track walking, I am unlikely to be able to venture far. To be honest I don't feel that drive to go climbing now that Jules is no longer here.

I still think of him nearly every day and the adventures we had. Often at night I dream of him, and it is always the same. We are climbing up a mountain out of the fog into sunshine. I can see those magnificent legs and just want to touch them and hold him in my arms.

I wake up with a smile and look towards the cot beside my bed. There is Julian kicking his little but already strong legs patiently waiting for his morning feed. I will always remember the day he was born being as it was exactly nine months to the day since his dad had died on Mt Aoraki.

Enchanted

by Jo Eden

Enchanted

Enchante smiled to herself as she listened to the finches chirping playfully in the crabapple tree above her. "That's a good one." She laughed gleefully. Bird's, especially finches, have a particularly good sense of humour. She wanted to tell the jokes to her parents, but she just didn't have the words to translate what they had said. The words just didn't exist in her vocabulary.

Although their only child had some 'special' abilities, Enchante's parents weren't perturbed. They too had some curious, slightly oddball aspects to themselves that set them apart at family gatherings. She was just part of a very atypical family.

Enchante eavesdropped on other birds too. She kept away from the black birds as they had a critical nature, and often made unkind observations about humans. She had also overheard some stinging remarks they had made about her. She enjoyed the company of fantails with their cheerful "cheet, cheet, cheet", though they made her feel a trifle insecure. Unlike the finches, their language was difficult for her to decipher. It was as if they spoke a loftier dialect. They were like some humans she had met, who appeared very friendly and agreeable, but as you walked away you had the uneasy feeling they were having a little snigger about you. Fantails, she thought, were well informed regarding humans. They knew a lot of things that humans didn't, and they weren't planning to share them.

Enchante didn't have many friends. Apparently, mothers warned their daughters to give her a wide berth. Because of this it seemed that solace for her loneliness was provided for her in other ways. It wasn't just the birds who spoke to Enchante. Other things did too, like the printer in the library at school. It called out names to her, often All Blacks names like "Weepu". It would say the word repeatedly as if it was trying to get her to do something. "Weepu, Weepu, Weepu." The water pump at home spoke to her too. It appeared to want the "wool cheque" and it too would repeat it over and over, "wool cheque, wool cheque, wool cheque." Even to a perceptive child such as Enchante, it was mystifying, especially as her family had a dairy farm.

Although school was a solitary experience for Enchante, spinning around in her own extraordinary orbit, she did have a few acquaintances that were always waiting for her when she got off the bus after school. I say acquaintances, as it was early days. The connection Enchante hoped for was not yet a reality. Some were quite bad-mannered. They just stood and stared at her, then raised their tail as if to let her know what they thought of her. She found this very insulting, so would try to only engage with the ones with kind eyes, those who showed her tricks like licking their nose with their tongues and flicking flies with their tails. She found they were incredibly good listeners, and talking to them helped her off-load after a lonely day at school. The Jersey cows were particularly attentive, their tender eyes unblinking as they hung on her every word. It appeared to Enchante that cows weren't big talkers. Only the occasional "there, there" or "never mind". However, the rhythmic chewing of their cuds soothed Enchantes fragile heart as if to say, "Chill out, nothing is worth getting too upset about." Still, she was lonely.

In breaks at school Enchante would, as is the custom of lonely people, hurry off to the library as if on a mission. This was to give the impression she had better things to do than hang about with the other girls giggling in the locker room. Mostly it was just her and Miss Purdoo, the librarian there.

Miss Purdoo sat straight as a ramrod, surveying the rows of books. Her nostrils flaring as if daring one of them to change places when she wasn't watching. She probably has trouble making friends too, thought Enchante caringly. Though she looked frightening, with a perpetual look of disdain on her face when she spoke with the children or other staff, she was a kind soul. Enchante wondered if Miss Purdoo's mother had told her not to pull faces like that, but she hadn't listened, and the wind had changed, so she had been stuck with it. Mothers are usually extremely wise. She thought too that it was a shame the hairdresser had cut her "bob" in such a way that it curled up towards her nose, which sadly bent down to meet it. Enchante had been afraid of Miss Purdoo, but over time, after spending so many lunch times together, they seemed to have developed an understanding. Enchante sat reading, hoping Miss Purdoo would have some printing to do. Sure enough, she didn't have to wait long. "Weepu, Weepu" went the printer, and Enchante smiled to herself. She looked up at Miss Purdoo. She could have sworn she saw the librarian's face soften a little and heard a sigh escape through her thin red lips

The next day Enchante sat at her desk doodling on her jotter pad as Mr. Dumdee droned on about Pythagoras. She watched reproachfully as a hail of paper pellets bounced off the back the teacher's tired, crumpled jacket while he wrote on the whiteboard. "Another lonely man," thought Enchante wistfully. There was a new boy in her class today, and she looked over to see if he was laughing with the other students at Mr. Dumdee. But he was gazing out the window, oblivious to the classroom antics, pleasing Enchante somewhat.

Finally, the lunch bell rang, and after she wolfed down her vegemite sandwiches, she made her escape to the library and waited for the printer to stir into life. Today Miss Purdoo had left her desk and was seated in the silent reading corner, resting her head on her hand, sighing from time to time. This is very odd, thought Enchante, whatever is the matter?

Miss Purdoo, who was a kind soul, as mentioned earlier, was thinking about Enchante. She was so like her when she was a child, Miss Purdoo reflected. She had been lonely too. Enchante is a kindred spirit, she smiled to herself. It's not good for a child to spend her free time at school alone in the library, waiting for the printer to talk to her. But what could she do to help the poor girl?

Enchante sat watching Miss Purdoo. Whatever is she doing now? This is most peculiar; she felt quite uneasy. Miss Purdoo was now over by the window and seemed to be watching something. Who was that sitting under the spreading ash tree? Miss Purdoo wrinkled her brow and squinted her eyes in concentration. That's where she sat with Mr. Dumdee after a weary day at school once the children had gone home, of course.

It was the new boy and what he was doing interested her very much. She looked over at Enchante. "My dear, have you met Edmund, the new boy?" Miss Purdoo nodded her head in the direction of the window. Enchante cautiously peered out. She took a long hard look, then with a shy smile at Miss Purdoo, she excused herself and made her way out into the school grounds and over to the ash tree. There was Edmund, the new boy, tossing his lunch crusts to the finches and laughing his head off as he listened to the chatter around him. Finches really do have the funniest sense of humour. As

Enchante joined Edmund under the tree, Miss Purdoo could be seen watching from the library window with a very amused, but satisfied smile on her face. She looked quite lovely.

For Love

by Nic Judson

About Nic

My world changed for the better in 2019 when I took up the NaNoWriMo (National Novel Writing Month) challenge to write 50,000 words in the month of November. I managed 30,000 and now I'm hooked.

I truly believe everybody has a story inside themselves. You just need the courage to get the words out and put them on paper and that challenge inspired me to write from the heart without fear. I haven't looked back.

For love

Ramone opened the thin kitchen curtains to let in the early morning light. He sat at the table with his plate of bacon and eggs in front of him.

As he brought a mouthful of egg to his mouth, speckles of yolk dropped onto his paperwork of his recent blood test. It glared back at him with defiance. The capital A ticked at him like a timebomb. He knew his parents were both B's. They were proud blood donors and their framed certificates on the wall indicated as such. He knew the math; he wasn't a dummy. He scooped up the remains of the egg with his bread and stuffed it into his mouth. He placed his knife and fork across his plate and waited.

His parents came down the stairs. His father headed out the front door and scuffed his slippers down the footpath to the mailbox to collect the paper. His mother put their coffee and toast on the table and sat opposite her son. The front door opened with a flourish and his father came walking in reading, the paper open as he walked.

"Found something interesting, dear?"

'Yes, they found that fisherman's body that went missing two weeks ago."

"His family will be relieved."

His father sat down next to his mother and sipped at his coffee.

Ramone looked over at his parents.

"I need to ask you both something."

"What is it, dear?"

His father still had his head behind the paper, and his mother began to butter her toast.

"Are you both my biological parents?"

His mother stopped buttering her toast and looked over at her husband. He had put the paper down and looked over at his wife. They looked at each other for some time. His father folded his paper over and placed it to one side and cleared his throat.

"We thought that this day would never happen, to be asked this question."

His father reached over and took his wife's hand.

"You need to know that we both love and adore you. That will never change, and we hope… that over time you may forgive us."

Ramone waved his blood test at his parents.

"I just want to know the truth. Why would I need to forgive you? I would still love you."

His mother started to cry, and his father gripped her hand tighter.

"As far as we are concerned, you are our son. We may not have a piece of paper to prove it, but you are still our son. Your mother and I couldn't have children. We only wanted to be parents. The adoption process was so long and tedious. We didn't want to wait."

"What are you trying to say, Dad?"

His father reached over to take his son's hand.

"We weren't thinking, but in our hearts we knew we were doing the right thing. The mother left you crying in your car seat. She didn't deserve to have you. We knew we could give you so much more love…"

My father broke down and cried.

"Please forgive us…."

Is it Safe?

by Nic Judson

Is it safe?

Emily picked her red ball gown off the floor and began to run down the spiral staircase. One of her silhouette heels caught on the 34th step and she slid and bounced and landed at the bottom with one final bounce onto the last step.

She rolled over onto her side and on her hands and knees got up off the floor. Luckily, she had no broken bones. She felt her backside with her hand and thought to herself that she would have a huge bruise tomorrow, but right now she didn't have time to consider what shade of blue it would be. She hobbled out to the street and walked down to her car which she had parked two blocks away. She dared not turn around. Within view of her car, she unlocked it and it bleeped at her out of the darkness. She opened the door and slammed it behind, punching the door locks at the same time. As she turned the ignition, nothing happened. Chills went down her spine. She flicked the engine hood and jumped out of the car and peered in with the glow of the torch on her phone. She gasped at the view before her. Someone had cut her starter cables! She rushed around to the driver seat and once again locked the door behind her before dialling his number.

"Victor speaking."

"It's me… I need your help."

There was silence on the end of the phone.

"Where are you?"

"On the corner of Pine and Main."

"Are you safe?"

"I'm locked in my car… he's tampered with the wiring."

Again, there was silence.

"Is it safe?"

"Yes, I have it with me."

"He'll be watching you. I'll come as fast as I can."

I looked through the driver's window into the darkness. There was a well-lit streetlamp up ahead. Under it was a parked car, and I could just make out an outline of a person inside.

"He's already here… I'm afraid."

"Stay on the phone."

I could hear Victor running and his car turn over.

"He's getting out of his car."

"I'm five minutes away."

I started to cry.

"He's just pulled out a gun."

"You know what you need to do."

My mind was racing. I knew in my heart Victor wouldn't have time to reach me. I reached into my handbag and pulled the sim card out. I couldn't let the man have it. I knew it was now or never. I popped it into my mouth and took a huge swallow.

"I've swallowed it."

Victor yelled down the phone.

"I'm coming around the corner, I can see him!"

The man's gun pointed at my head through the driver's window.

"I think it's too late... I love you."

I knew this was a recipe for disaster when I took on this job, but I didn't think it would end like this.

The Wicked Witch of Butterscotch Lane

by Nic Judson

The Wicked Witch of Butterscotch Lane

The tall, willowy silver birches shimmered in the brisk summer evening. Their leaves jostled for attention, crying out, 'look at me, look at me!' Shrieking magpies flew overhead as a paperboy scuttered past on his bike, throwing with glee the evening paper into the prickly holly hedge. The boy sped faster on his chopper bike as he spied movement from one of the front windows. Curtain movement, ever so slightly, from the front bay window.

Sat within was Mrs Peebottom, a grey-haired widow who collected buttons, but to everyone else in this neighbourhood, including the paperboy, she was the wicked witch of Butterscotch Lane. The only child who had dared to step close to her front door and get a glimpse of the wicked witch, was never to be seen again, or so the rumour went.

The only sign of life was on a Saturday evening when all was dark and Mrs Peebottom would peer out her window to make sure no-one else was around, before hobbling out to the pavement and hopping into her Volkswagen beetle, coloured red, with rust holes peeking through the bonnet. She would jam a dark blue hat on her head, grip the steering wheel and grind the gears into first, leaving a whirl of dust in her wake. She would be halfway up the street before throttling the gears into second. Only Thomas, her neighbour, would ever see her come home again after his night shift, at 4 am. He would hide in the shadows behind his hedge just to get a peek to see if she really was a wicked witch. He could only imagine what she would get up to at this ungodly hour.

One Sunday morning after seeing the wicked witch get out of her car, she stumbled and fell heavily onto the pavement. Thomas, looking around and wondering if he should go to her assistance, found his right leg making the first step across the street. He reached down and gingerly pulled the wicked witch up off the ground. Mrs Peebottom stumbled on her feet, so Thomas found himself using his arms to guide her up her front path and into her front door. The door swung shut behind him.

"Could you guide me to my couch in the parlour, young man?" soothed Mrs Peebottom. Thomas walked her gently to the couch, and Mrs Peebottom flopped down amongst the cushions. She pointed to her foot stool, and Thomas moved it over so she could place her feet on top.

"Can I get you anything, ur, umm, wit... Mrs?"

"A nice cup of tea would be grand, young man."

After a time, Thomas came back into the parlour with a hot cup of tea for Mrs Peebottom. It was at this time Thomas decided to find his courage and asked the wicked witch why she came home so late on a Sunday morning all the time.

"Well, young man.... or perhaps you have a name?"

"Thomas."

"Pleased to meet you Thomas, my name is Kathryn."

So it was that Kathryn told her story of why she came home so late to an enthralled Thomas, who sat alongside her on the couch.

Unknown Texter

by Liz Cook

About Liz

In 2015 my husband and I shifted to Ashburton from Christchurch.

I have only recently joined the Ashburton Writers Group. I always loved writing stories when I was younger, so it is a mixture of fun and a challenge to be putting pen to paper, creating stories and poems.

Unknown Texter

It's only 6.30am. I can't seem to get out of the habit of waking early. It's been six months since Bob died suddenly, and I still can't sleep past the time he used to get up and go to work.

The house is so quiet, after the last few weeks, hectic with family staying for Christmas. Keep yourself busy they said. Get out and join some clubs. Easy for them to say. Though I should do something to make an effort, after all I did make a New Year's resolution to make some changes and be more adventurous.

I'll have a play with the cellphone Michael gave me for Christmas. He explained in detail all about it, and I think I must have nodded in all the right places because he seemed happy that I knew what I was doing. Hmmm, if he only knew – went in one ear and out the other. Though he did leave some notes. I'll get them out.

Well, none of this makes sense. I can't get the damn thing to work. I don't really want to go down to the shop and admit to those young things that I can't use it.

Back to the instructions and make sure I go step by step. I think I've finally turned it on. There's the place to click for calling. There are my emails. Not that I get many. Oh, and there is where I send texts. Though who on earth I will be contacting I don't know. Still, I could text Michael and let him know I am trying.

"Bing!" Oh, what have I done? I didn't touch anything. There is a 1 on the message box. I click the message. What the?? "Meet me outside now."

What do I do? No, don't think. I wanted some excitement and to be spontaneous. I will go outside and see who knows.

As I get to the gate a car pulls up and a man gets out, opens the car door and tells me to get in. He looks a bit dodgy and keeps looking around.

Both him and the driver are in dark suits wearing dark sunglasses. I feel like I am in a scene from Men in Black. An alien abduction? Perhaps I've been a bit hasty.

How stupid could I be? Neither of them seem keen on conversation. I suppose the best thing to do is to take note of as much as I can. I try and think what Miss Marple would do.

I have been so lost in thought I haven't noticed where we are going. Really panicked now. I don't recognise anywhere.

Breathe. I resign myself to having been so stupid, and if I get out of this alive, which I doubt, I won't be so eager to be adventurous.

We seem to have been driving for ages and are now pulling up outside a warehouse. No one else is around that I can see.

The younger man opens the door and motions me to get out. I wonder what he would do if I refused? Probably not a good idea, he looks a bit thuggish.

I hop out and he nudges me towards a door. I really start to question my sanity now, but I won't give them the satisfaction of me crying. I'm sure they have the wrong person, but it's a bit late to tell them now.

It is dark inside and they push me into a chair. All of a sudden, the lights flash on and a big yell of surprise. I nearly have heart failure. Michael and the family all there. Laughing at the look on my face.

Michael comes up and hugs me, whispering, "I heard your resolution and thought I could give you a bit of excitement on your birthday. Though I wasn't sure if you would get in the car."

I didn't know whether to hug or hit him. That was enough excitement to last me a lifetime. Though I am waiting for the lectures about being so stupid from my daughter. Well, I'm not going to let that spoil my party.

Christmas Recipe

by Liz Cook

Christmas Recipe

Christmas is coming
How can we miss it
The ads, the sales
I just want to diss it
All so commercial and aimed at selling
The old Christmas story
No-one is telling
My turn it is to host Christmas Day
So a pot luck it is
What's that you say?
No organised menu
Just bring what you feel
Whatever it is will be a good meal
For me a Trifle is what I will do
Sponge and Peaches
Jelly, Sherry and Custard
Something simple
Easily done and dusted
Some prep is involved the day before making
I sample the sherry and get started baking
Get the Jelly in the fridge, the custard made

Another sherry, I'm well on the way
Christmas Eve arrives
The jelly is set
And the custard cooled
My trifle bowl all sparkling and gleaming
Another sherry down and I am beaming
So out comes the sponge
I am ready to cut, dip and soak
Remember too much sherry can make people choke
So mix it with juice
Add peaches and jelly
A layer of custard
Too much, not on your Nelly
But what amounts are needed I hear you ask
I'm not bothered with those I just get on with the task
Bowl only half full so continue I do
More layers I add
Though only a few
Finally, a sight to behold
The colours red and green so bold
Back in the fridge my creation goes
The actual flavour I do not know
It's Christmas morning and excitement is mounting
It's such a relief there will be no more counting
The family and friends all start to arrive
A much-needed drink after a very long drive
My trifle is ready to take centre stage
Ready to be enjoyed by any age

Be in quick there are those that don't share
For those that don't like trifle
So many sherries I don't really care

$\mathcal{DNA}$

by Liz Cook

DNA

I am so excited. I actually got onto the project. My friends say I am officially a nerd now. Can't wait to tell Mum and Dad. This might be my ticket into Uni and the science degree I want to do.

I get home to a quiet house and because I'm first home I will surprise the olds with dinner. While it is cooking, I sort out the stuff in my backpack.

Three DNA kits and the paperwork for the research project. Looking at DNA and the genetics of how two people's DNA make another human.

This is going to be so interesting. I don't actually look like either of my parents, but I've been told I take after some old great aunt that I never met. Thinking about it, I don't think I have ever seen a photo either. Oh well.

Here's Mum, looking a bit tired, but I will wait for Dad to come home and let them chill out a bit before I tell them all about it. I'm sure they will be so excited for me and more than willing to do their bit.

It seems neither of them had a particularly good day, but I'm sure this will cheer them up. They always want me to do well.

Dinner's over and dishes sorted. Mum and Dad are settled in the lounge with their wines.

I go in and mute the TV. I must look a bit nervous because Mum asks what is wrong. Dad is just a bit shitty because he can't listen to the news.

I take a breath and just launch into it – the big explanation. I am so into the whole thing, that to start with, I don't notice that they aren't having the reaction I expected. Both of them have gone pale. Mum looks like she wants to be sick. Dad is just staring at the floor looking stunned.

I slowly stop talking and just look at them. I am really confused. Where is their excitement? They haven't jumped up to hug me. What is their problem? Is it perhaps they think the DNA test is an invasion of their privacy? Or perhaps they don't want big brother having their personal details?

Mum looks at Dad. She looks like somebody has died or something. I start to say that the test is quite simple and not invasive, but Mum stops me.

She takes a breath and starts crying. In between sobs she says that they can't do the test as it won't help me. What the…

What on earth is she talking about? I sit down and try and concentrate on what she is saying.

They were travelling through Europe…yeah, I know they had done an OE. They were in Romania and they helped in an orphanage. So what? Apparently, they fell in love with me.

What? I am adopted? And not even a Kiwi? How can you not have told me?

It seems there was never any info that identified my biological parents, so they have no idea of any family or history about me.

I feel like I am in a B movie. I feel like my whole life has been a lie. They never told me because it never seemed the right time.

I don't know how to deal with this. Mum is talking about counselling, but I really don't know where to start.

In this Neighbourhood

by Liz Cook

In this Neighbourhood

Well at last hubby has a new job
A good step up that brings in a few extra bob
Trouble is we will need to shift
Always a hassle if you get my drift
In a new town we will have to look
Time to get out the real estate book
So many questions to be sorted
But it won't beat me
I won't be thwarted
Do we want a townhouse
Or a Grand Villa
With a family of four we will soon fill her
Hours and hours with agents spent
I sometimes wish we could just rent
Narrowed it down to a choice of two
In different suburbs not sure what to do
Drive around the townhouse area
All these decisions it couldn't be scarier
Might be an idea to stop and talk to a resident
Happens to be the Ratepayer Association President
Friendly people, plenty of parks, cafes and shops

With an auction looming we need to pull out all stops
In this neighbourhood the kids would be close to school
They could go by themselves
They would think that was cool
Off we go in the other direction
A grand old villa with a huge section
Trying to be practical I look at the house
A bit rundown so DIY it will need
Hubby's not so handy I have to concede
In this neighbourhood there are treelined streets
The train is close so that is sweet
Something is missing though as I look around
There is not any everyday sound
In the street it is extraordinarily quiet
So on reflection don't think we will buy it
To this area I am quite ambivalent
It seems house one has no equivalent
Contact the agent, the bank and solicitor
For the auction we need to register
Auction day and we are all ready
The bids go up nice and steady
My heart is racing as the hammer falls
The house is ours the agent calls
In this neighbourhood the chosen one
The kids can play outside till the day is done
At the stream at the park
Even the dog will have fun and be able to bark
For us adults there is the restaurant and bar

It will be great we won't need the car
We can pop down for an afternoon reviver
Without the need for a sober driver
In this neighbourhood we couldn't do better
Oh look there's a neighbour
All smiles and greetings
I'm sure this is the first of many meetings.

Grief

by Tania Scott

About Tania

Tania Scott writes short stories and poems; she has also worked as a feature writer for a community newspaper.

Tania has two children, two cats, two dogs, two sheep and one husband. She lives in a small moveable home in a local riverbed and, despite having wandering feet, is fiercely loyal to the Ashburton District.

Her work as a psychologist influences her writing, which reflects her curiosity about the human mind.

Grief

"Handle with Care"
The smug sticker on a manila box,
Which lies turd-like on the desk.
Don't look at me.

If she had been wearing that advisory label a week ago,
would we even be here?
Avoiding, accusing, saying goodbye,
I wouldn't follow her instructions anyway – too hollow.
A dried wheaten, brow beaten, wind-blown, slightly
more than dust, husk.

Not as insubstantial as ash
Not nothing, but teeth and bone in a jam jar,
Undercover of a box with a conspiratorial sticker
Addressing me, waiting, for me to own it.
Standing, an elephant, in the middle of the room
Don't talk to me.

Now what?
Take her home? Care and dear for her?

Hold her close and share with her?
You know I am not equipped for that dutiful role.

I don't want a jar
It would sure as shit shatter, not that it matters.
The damage is done. I miss my mum.
Dam cracking, face flushed, eyes flutter.
Grief roars, soaking the walls like the cry of a baby
Don't listen to me.

What can you do?
A raw bare bone salted wound sucking,
And sniffling, around that plain clothed box with its
ironic sticker
Are you uncomfortable with my despair?
Follow the instruction
"Handle with care"

The Slip Up

by Tania Scott

The Slip Up

Rudy was going to burst, sweat beaded on his forehead as his stomach cramped again. He paused shovelling; he could probably dig for another ten minutes, but hey —who was he trying to please? Heaving himself out of the pit, he looked over at the old hooker, it was a pity really. Rudy remembered when Trixie arrived on the street. She had been keen and ready for adventure. He sighed; street life was hard, it aged you quickly. Trixie was all used up and now she had to disappear.

Rudy grasped the barrel of his abdomen, he was exploding and he was going to have to take a dump right here in the park. Ripping his pants down, he was oblivious to anything but his own intestinal circus. He certainly didn't notice Trixie roll over and clamber onto all fours, nor did he notice her shakily reaching for the shovel he had hastily dropped. He may have noticed the shovel arc down towards his skull or he may have been cursing his poor choice of lunch, and then Rudy didn't notice anything at all.

Trixie had been more or less dead for the last 24 hours, and she was now only more or less alive. She shuffled to the fat man's van and found the keys in it.

There wouldn't be any drugs but there might be a gun. Trixie needed a gun more than she needed a fix because the Geezer would kill her again when he found her. But she did desperately want a fix, and she wondered if crazy Ben was peddling in his usual spot by the park gate. She edged the van onto the quiet tree-lined avenue creeping towards the exit. At the gate she called Ben over.

When Ben saw Trixie, he began to shake. A humming started in his head. What did the ghost want? Living, Trixie had always been hungry, gobbling anything he had. Reaching into his bag, Ben held out a synthetic joint and saw Trixie nod tiredly. He climbed into the van passing it to her, careful not to touch her.

Trixie inhaled greedily, feeling an instant hit. She immediately sucked more of the chemical cocktail. Trixie may have found Nirvana in that second toke, or she may have cursed the relentless need of her addiction, but now Trixie wouldn't want anything ever again.

Crazy Ben took the gun; his head was roaring with agitated voices, and he needed to getaway. He lifted the gun and became a hero in an action movie weaving through the park, feeling more useful than he ever had. Ben tripped on something soft and went cartwheeling. He didn't intend to squeeze the trigger, and as the gun kicked savagely in his hand, Ben thought being a hero wasn't for him anymore. He left the gun in the pit and climbed out.

The Geezer had heard Ben shouting among the trees and wondered if anyone would put that crazy kid out of his misery. He also wondered where the fuck Rudy was and if that last batch of synthetic had too much rat poison in it. The Geezer was wondering if killing Trixie had been worth the bother when the bullet ripped through his throat, and the Geezer never wondered about his mistakes again.

Reimagined Fairy Tale

by Tania Scott

Reimagined Fairy Tale

Once upon a modern time two children were pushed out of their home by their narcissistic stepfather. Their mother had developed depression several years ago and could no longer get out of bed to care for her children.

The school had sent a truancy officer regarding absenteeism, the local shopping mall sent the police regarding petty theft, and the church had sent a minister regarding smoking in the cemetery. The stepfather, having no patience for the do-gooder intrusions into his life, and hoping to instill a life lesson for the delinquent tweens, drove them to the middle of the city and abandoned them there. Hansel whispered to his sister not to be scared as he had their mother's phone and could use Google maps to get home.

The city was dark and scary, but Gretel felt safe with her brother. She was starting to get hungry though and the children had no money to purchase any food. It was a blessing when they saw an old woman giving food to a line of people. Each person got a bowl of soup and a bun. Hansel and Gretel quickly joined the queue. When they finally reached the front, their mouths were watering and their hands shaking. The old woman felt their bony trembling hands and said to the children to take their soup inside, as there were biscuits and cake for afterwards.

Hansel and Gretel couldn't believe their luck and raced inside the brightly painted building. No sooner were the children through the door when it was slammed shut and locked. Gretel turned to Hansel, terrified, begging him to use the phone to get help, but alas it was out of credit and the Wi-Fi was a secure network.

However, the old lady had not lied when she said the room was filled with cakes, biscuits and breads. It smelt heavenly with the best smells coming from the large still-warm oven.

The children took small bites of everything, with each baked item more delicious than the last. Until Hansel warned his sister to stop eating as he worried she would throw up. This gave Gretel an idea.

"When the old bat comes back let's pretend we ate too much."

So, when the tired lady finally returned to the room, the children were rolling on the floor holding their stomachs and moaning. She rushed to aid them. Immediately, Gretel leapt up and opened the oven door while Hansel shoved the old woman with all his might so that she fell backwards into the oven.

"Wait," she cried, "Oranga Tamariki are on their way to help."

The children shouted "Witch." They slammed the oven door shut on the social worker and ran out into the street where they were welcomed, and they soon became part of the community who lived there.

In this Neighbourhood

by Julie Fechney

About Julie

Hello there, I'm Julie Fechney, President of the Ashburton Writers' Group.

I joined about five years ago, looking for something creative to do. I loved writing at school and thought, 'why not?' What I didn't expect was the laughter and friendships that I have made.

The two stories that I have submitted for this book were both prompted by our monthly assignments. 'Date night' was written in about half an hour, on the day of the meeting; organisation isn't my middle name, of which everyone in the group knows and has me on about.

'In this Neighbourhood' is based on stories that my daughter would tell me about living in a cul-de-sac in Upper Riccarton during her University days. I'll let you decide which stories are true, as real life is stranger than fiction!

In this Neighbourhood

Dear Madge,

I hope you and your family are all well and thriving. Since our last correspondence, situations in the neighbourhood have gone to rack and ruin.

The single mother at number 19 caused such a scene the other night. She threw her boarder—and I use that term very loosely—out of her house. Threw his clothes out onto the street and proceeded to tell him in very colourful language what he could do to himself. According to Sally at number 21, he had been seeing the young lady at number 32.

The young skater boy fell off his skateboard and managed to break his wrist, but that has not stopped him from whizzing around the neighbourhood, with a sense of entitlement, that only the young now seem to think is their right.

The police have once again visited the two young women at number 15, who are on home detention, so I found out from Gaye at number 13. I wonder if someone tipped them off that they have been dealing in meth, as she explained to me. Why anyone would buy methylated spirits from them and not the hardware store is a mystery to me. Perhaps it is cheaper?

Jim is still pursuing me by dropping hints that perhaps having lunch together at the pub might be nice. While the senior citizen menu of roast of the day and an ice cream sundae to finish might seem good; sharing a mealtime with such a boring man, whose conversation centres around the television programmes that he watches, is just not my cup of tea.

The neighbourhood rabbit is still being evasive. Now, he has taken up residence in my hedge. The children next door swear that it is their pet rabbit that got away, but I am not convinced. If they treat their pets the way they treat each other, then all I can say is well done to the rabbit for having the foresight to get away.

Anyway, time for me to end this letter and go and investigate the banging that is going on at number 25. A new couple moved in last week and a steady stream of tradesmen have been coming and going.

Kind regards, your best friend,

Ethel

Date Night

by Julie Fechney

Date Night

She sat at the bar pondering, while sipping on a Martini, how in the world it took more than two hours to get ready. Hair done, full makeup and wearing her newly purchased little black dress, she felt like another woman, not the mother of two who worked full-time to provide for her little family.

Tonight, she was cutting loose. The children were at their grandparents for the weekend, so it was the ideal time for her to have "adult" time. The cute bartender had kept an eye on her drink and who sat next to her. Any lewd looks from fellow male patrons were met with an icy cold "don't you dare" stare.

The bar itself was situated on the ground floor of a 5-star hotel. Just enough wood panelling to make the place feel enclosing and warm. Just the right amount of lighting to see what you were drinking, and the soft jazz piped through the speakers, made the bar quite an experience. No blue-collar workers here, just a few couples meeting for drinks after work and the occasional single male who dared to sit next to her and strike up a conversation.

She took another sip as her phone vibrated. Picking up her clutch off the bar, she retrieved her phone, hoping it wasn't a text from her parents saying that a child was sick and could she come home, but no, it was a text from an unknown number asking her to meet her in the lobby, now!

She didn't answer but put the phone back in the clutch, picked up her compact mirror and did a final check of her makeup. The butterflies were not settling in her stomach, so she downed the last of the Martini and placed the empty glass on the bar top. Hopping off the stool, she pulled down her little black dress and walked confidently out of the bar and into the lobby.

She scanned the area and found the chair where someone was reading the paper. She knew by the fingers holding the paper that it was a man, and this was her "date". She walked up to him and with her index finger pulled the middle of the paper down, thinking that this was the best way to get his attention.

At that moment, she wished the ground would swallow her up. It wasn't the man she thought it would be. Instead of the handsome, dark haired, early 40ish husband, there sat an ageing, going bald rather quickly man. His Cheshire cat grin told the woman that he certainly enjoyed the view.

Her breath left her, and she felt faint for a few seconds until the man produced an envelope.

"This is what you need," he said as he handed it to her, stood, winked, and started to walk towards the front door.

Putting the clutch under her right arm, she tore open the envelope and peered inside. She picked up a hotel key chain with the number 425 on it. No note was included, but as she stood there, she smiled and laughed to herself.

Trust her husband to make this night one of adventure. It was his idea that she dressed to kill and that they would meet at the bar, have dinner, and stay the night at the hotel. A little vacation without leaving the city.

'Perhaps' she thought, to herself as she walked to the lift, 'baby number three might have to be named Hilton'.

Tomorrow is a New Day

by Julie Fechney

Tomorrow is a New Day

Tomorrow is a new day filled with love and laughter,
Where all the challenges fade
to make the future brighter.

Focus on the road ahead,
Don't waste time looking back
Because the past is gone and won't return
So keep your dreams on track.

Set your goals and go for them
And reach for the stars.
Be what everyone else knows –
That you are a gem!!

The members of the Ashburton Writers Group would like to thank you for purchasing this copy of

Group Therapy.

Helping us to support Hospice Mid Canterbury.